68 Via Condotti
Book One - Eternity Ltd.

A. G. Hayes

Savant Books and Publications
Honolulu, HI, USA
2019

Published in the USA by Savant Books and Publications
2630 Kapiolani Blvd #1601
Honolulu, HI 96826
http://www.savantbooksandpublications.com

Printed in the USA

Edited by Daniel S. Janik
Cover by Daniel S. Janik

13 digit ISBN: 9780999463345

First Edition: March 2019
Library of Congress Control Number: 2018914995

Acknowledgements

Acknowledgements are traditionally for those playing a significant part in the creation, editing, proofing and/or publicity of a work for which they receive no monetary compensation.

Every written story, no matter how small or large is typically the end product of hours of discussion. As authors, friends, colleagues and co-researchers, Raymond Gaynor and I spent many pleasant hours over the phone imagining and re-imagining the characters, plot and storyline for this 1950's serial movie style three-book set, featuring Kate Keenan, a strong female protagonist introduced to Koski and Falk in FINDING KATE (Savant 2016). Kate, upon Falk's recommendation, found a place in Cerebrus alongside Koski and Falk as a special assignment agent in QUANTUM DEATH (Savant 2016). In this, her third appearance, Kate comes into her own in one of the most complex and intriguing operations yet. All this without receiving any salary income from me or my publisher. So, thanks, Kate Keenan, Susan Koski, Joseph Falk and, my dear friend, Raymond Gaynor, who, if he were a character would be standing staunchly alongside my others in making these adventures to life.

Foreword

Having had the privilege of working with A. G. Hayes on his sixth Koski and Falk installment, QUANTUM DEATH (Savant 2016), I feel doubly privileged to write a foreword to what I personally consider one of his best works to date: his three-book, 68 Via Condotti Series beginning with this first book entitled 68 VIA CONDOTTI: BOOK ONE - ETERNITY LTD.

This series represents a synthesis of many of A. G. Hayes' more wildly imagined and here-to-fore unpublished stories. The third in the Kate Keenan Special Assignment series, it connects back with her introduction in FINDING KATE (Savant 2016) and her further development in QUANTUM DEATH (Savant 2016), elevating Kate to independent special agent status and placing her in the center of one of the most complex Cerberus operations yet.

A particularly interesting aspect of this 50's-style movie-like serial, is Hayes' unrelenting exploration of what it means to be human. Others have attempted to tackle this Gordian Knot, but there's something in his unique approach to this question in this three-book progression that significantly raises the bar and opens the door (some might to a Pandora's Box) surrounding an understanding of what makes humans -- but not necessarily highly intelligent robots or even aliens -- human.

This is an adventure-suspense-mystery-espionage thriller in every sense of the words, but it's also a mature exploration into the soul of humanity. Go, Kate, go, but be sure to watch your back and trust no one!

- Raymond Gaynor

Prologue

In 1977, Pope Paul VI wrote a personal missive largely unknown to the outside world in which he voiced an anguished warning that eventually caused shock and scandal within the Catholic world: "...through some crack, the smoke of Satan has entered the Church of God."

Father Gabriele Amorth of the Society of St. Paul, a lesser known order of the Church devoted to communicating the Christian message using all possible technological means, the founder and honorary president of the International Association of Exorcists, was busy researching a new kind of possession: anomalies in computers, robotics, artificial intelligence, and electronics, that, without warning, were resulting in "erratic performance"—blackouts, crashes and other non-traceable breakdowns that were becoming a mounting problem, not only for the Catholic Church but the world, and, more specifically, its various international intelligence agencies.

On the twenty-eighth of February 2013, the Pope that Father Gabriele Amorth currently served, Pope Benedict XVI, abruptly resigned, publicly citing his advancing age as the reason. According to anonymous Vatican officials, he would remain sequestered in Vatican City in order to provide him "security and protection" from potential lawsuits.

Subsequently, an emissary of the U.S. National Security Agency (NSA) secretly flew to Rome to meet with The Grand Master of the Sovereign Military Order of Malta in his office at 68 Via Condotti, from which the Order directs diplomatic relationships with over 100 countries, as well as the United Nations through a permanently established observer seat. The Grand Master, known colloquially as the Black Pope, controls the Church's relations with the world's intelligence services, including the United States' NSA, CIA, FBI and DIA, Great Britian's MI-5 and EU's Interpol, to name a few. This secret "Unified International Intelligence Community" which had come into being during Rome's Second Thirty Year War (1914-1945) and was used during the Cold War (1945-to present day) was about to reach a new pinnacle...

Chapter 1

A shaft of watery sunlight shone through the massive, vertical, stained-glass window of The Academy of Science building in the Vatican gardens. The beam reflected on a small crystal pyramid that Father Enrico Conti S. J. (for Society of Jesus, members being commonly called Jesuits) used as a paperweight.

Dan Blake moved his head slightly to lessen the reflection, and, Fr. Conti, noticing, pushed the crystal to one side. The briefing had been going on for almost an hour.

"Daniel, you and a select few representing intelligence agencies around the world have finally completed a most secret and rigorous program of specialized training here at the Vatican under the direction of The Grand Master of the Sovereign Military Order of Malta. With that training at hand, and the reason for that training now clear to you, I know you will do well. However, remember, no matter whom you think you can trust," Fr. Conti spread his fingers wide on the desktop, "always think twice, and take extra precautions because you are going to meet situations that at times will be beyond anything you have been taught about here or experienced in your life to date. The way you think and react to these various situations will undoubtedly tax you heavily. You are going into the future, always remember that."

"That I will, Sir," Blake said as he shifted uneasily in the hard wooden chair.

Fr. Conti continued. "This last year, you and other select members of different intelligence agencies from around the world were given this advanced training to address the results of two realities that were totally unknown to the world until a few years ago: one, the explosive growth of the science of artificial intelligence, and, two, existence of alien intelligence. I fear our world is in great peril, Daniel."

Daniel Blake leaned forward to receive Father Conti's blessing.

Chapter 2

Daniel Blake had attended Cambridge University, graduating with a first at age twenty-four. The majority of his university friends had since gone into academia, assuming he would, too. When he informed them of his decision to enter the Royal Military Academy Sandhurst, they were shocked.

Graduating from Sandhurst as a subaltern second lieutenant, he joined a Guards regiment, and a year later applied for the Special Air Service, in due time attaining the rank of major. His ten years of service included stints in Iraq and Afghanistan eventually resulting in a growing number of private assignments for various security companies around the globe. These companies were continuously seeking men with talents such as his: intelligence, ruthlessness, a diversity of killing skills. When contacted by the Vatican through the Sovereign Military Order of Malta, he was at first speechless. Now, after intense indoctrination and training, and the blessing of the Holy See, he was ready to leave Rome and travel to

Wales on his first and according to his handler, Fr. Conti, the single most important assignment of his life. His cover was to be that of an ex-British army officer writing his memoirs and living on a small boat moored in a marina in Holyhead, Wales, UK.

Less than an hour later, he was climbing aboard a private jet on his way to the UK. As he settled in his seat, a signal was sent from the Vatican to MI-5 informing the agency that Operation Eternity was now in effect.

Two weeks later, a blast of light from a nearby lighthouse somehow found a way through a boat's constantly closed curtains, briefly illuminating the dingily lighted interior. An always present liability of nights on board a boat, Dan repositioned the curtains, closing them tighter. Returning to the galley stove, he switched it off, poured the boiling water into a metal teapot, cut a pork pie in half, stuffed it in his mouth and chewed thoughtfully. Having lived on board since his arrival in UK, the interior of the thirty-foot Essex sailboat seemed to be constantly shrinking, and now felt the size of a rowboat.

As he filled a mug with tea, his cell phone chirped; he listened, afterwards replying, "I'll meet her there." The brass chronometer positioned over a small navigation table showed 2015 hours. Taking a quick sip of the tea, he parted a nearer set of curtains, gazed across the marina and whispered, "Show time," eyeing his battered transport, a supercharged Mini

Cooper specially built to appear like a rusty, rundown beater, painted a splotchy primer gray with cosmetic rust spots added to complete the camouflage.

The bar of the Prince of Wales Pub in Holyhead was a zoo. Friday night, jammed with locals creating a noise level ideal for defeating any listening devices that might be in use, Dan Blake tuned it all out to locate an attractive blonde, Dr. Gwyneth Evans from among the crowd, sipping a lemon and lime at the bar. When Dan drew up to the bar and ordered a scotch and soda, she nodded toward a nearby couple preparing to leave their table. The two had to move fast, she sitting faster and grinning at him as he slid into the booth beside her.

"Well done," she said in a clipped British accent. Dan grinned, noting the way her pale blonde hair framed her face, accentuating her haunting green eyes. She was a beauty.

"How was your meeting with Father Funes?"

Dan shrugged. "Fine; he was getting ready to return to the Vatican Observatory at Castel Gandolfo. He mentioned he would be going to the Vatican's Advanced Technology Telescope and the annual seminar at the University of Arizona's Steward Observatory at Mount Graham later this year, and hoped we could visit him there."

"That would be great. Think there's any chance?"

"Father Funes stated obliquely that 'all being well', we would both meet him at the seminar." Dan set his glass down and lowered his voice. "He also said you'd bring me up to date on a meeting with Chadron."

The woman crinkled her eyes, producing an impish smile. "Yes. Monday evening at the Alan Turing Building, University of Manchester. Chadron will be there with me."

"Exactly who is this Chadron?"

"Let's just say a friend of mine with whom I think you'll be impressed. Together you two can both appreciate and enjoy the symposium on humanoid robotics and all the various aspects of mechatronic design, including electronic drives and bio-mechanical gears, sensors, software architecture, control, communications and their overarching cognitive issues."

Gwen swirled her drink. "There'll be guest speakers who will outline the design aspects of an unique, integrated robotic entity, as well as other presentations focusing on planned research studies based on the entity." Designed to be one-cubic meter in volume, the creation of the various parts of the open source robot were accomplished through a multi-national, multi-university RobotCub Consortium. Integrating these aspects together into one entity was the charge of the Italian Institute of Technology with, of course, the financial and technical support of several anonymous corporate giants. The result, fondly called iCub, had already sparked a worldwide explosion of research and development in humanoid robotics. Dan noticed Gwen's eyes shine at the thought. "An exhibition featuring the entity in action is planned during the symposium, allowing time for delegates to become familiar with its capabilities."

"There you are, then," Dan said with forced gaiety. "We can make an evening of it." He hated it when she assumed her all-business style of communication. Nonetheless, that was Gwyneth Evans, internationally renown academician and bionic skeletal expert.

After they finished their drinks, each left separately, Gwen to her car and, five minutes later, Dan to his and the marina where he mulled over the new approach the Vatican was formulating to accommodate non-human intelligent beings in the world. It was time for him to head to London.

A. G. Hayes

Chapter 3

Kate Keenan Ph.D. jerked awake at the sound of the landing gear lowering. Pushing up her window blind, she peered out at a thick bank of grey clouds. As her plane prepared to land at Heathrow, her thoughts flashed back to the phone call assigning her to report to the London office of the U. S. Defense Intelligence Agency.

In the bar in Heathrow's Terminal 5, Jack Drummond, a pinched-faced MI-5 agent, sipped coffee and watched the pulsating dot on his his GPS Bio-Tag scanner. Kate Keenan was the source of the signal. He spoke quietly into his iPhone: "She'll be on the ground in five minutes." Among the first to be field-trained in Bio-Tag technology, Drummond was pleased to finally be putting it to use.

He recalled his instructor holding out his hand to the class, palm up, saying, "Okay, lean in close, people," displaying what looked like a grain of brown rice. "Your subject will have ingested this device. Once swallowed, it sends out tendrils and attaches itself to their digestive tract. It will transmit a GPS signal for up to seventy-two hours after which it detaches and is passed. The signal can be accurately located anywhere on the planet to within five feet—even inside buildings."

London was as gray and wet as the view from her airplane window, a confusion of umbrellas, puddles, and a steady drift of rain. Kate's taxi pulled away in a cloud of spray, leaving her outside the Eccleston Hotel, tote bag on shoulder, dragging a wheeled suitcase. The doorkeeper called, "Hold hard, Miss, be right with you." Together, they climbed the steps to the entrance beneath the cover of his massive black umbrella.

"Looks like our rain caught you unprepared," he gasped, pushing the heavy ornate door open with a shove of his hip, at the same time snapping the huge umbrella shut. Kate made a mental note to get an umbrella of her own.

After checking in, a bellhop took Kate's rollaway and led the way to her room. Old fashioned, but recently renovated and comfortable, Kate tossed her bag on the bed, headed for the bathroom and looked in the mirror. Jet lag stared back. After a shower, shampoo, blow-dry and a few dabs of makeup, she returned to the main room and crossed to the window. Below, Eccleston square, a small private park with immaculately kept grounds, was flanked on three sides by eighteenth-century homes, each white-fronted and five stories, topped with gray slate roofs and assorted chimneys.

She blinked her pale blue eyes a couple of times assuring herself she was actually in London. Her mind reeled back several months to the offer by the US Defense Intelligence Agency asking if she would be interested in applying her knowledge of computer science to work with them on an especially perplexing problem. DIA was fully aware of a past situation in which she had successfully escaped from an underground movie film vault on a Hollywood back lot after being held captive and almost killed while making her escape from an autonomous intelligent robot. It all stemmed from a computer program Kate had created that was destined to revolutionize moviemaking, putting today's studios out of business. Hollywood and Bollywood wanted her and her computer program to vanish. Her work during that time had cost the loss of her fiancé and very nearly her father. On recommendation by Joseph Falk, a field agent for a clandestine international special operations agency, she was hired by that agency, Cerebrus, displaying exceptional courage and initiative in Operation Quantum Death in which, marshaling all her scientific knowledge, she was able to reverse the crippling effects of a quantum death machine, and literally save the United States from destruction. The US government had since come to realize her knowledge and abilities constituted a vital tool for use not only by Cerebrus, but also by the Defense Department. It all seemed so long ago…

Her London assignment was to go undercover for DIA as a reporter working for an up-and-coming Euro business magazine, meaning, of course, that she would need to look the part. She checked her watch and decided to explore a bit and purchase a raincoat and umbrella. There was still time before the shops closed.

When asked, the concierge recommended the Burlington Arcade on Bond Street adding, "If you enjoy antique shops, there's one on a narrow side street opposite the Arcade. I can't recall the street name, but you cannot miss it. You might find a good buy on an umbrella there."

Kate smiled, saying she loved antiquing and would check it out. The concierge offered to call a taxi. Outside, rain was now coming down hard. Kate replied yes.

Kate's taxi alternated between fast and slow as it weaved through the wet streets. At one point, the driver squeezed his black cab between two red double-decker buses—another coat of paint and they would have never made it. After the excitement, she sat back to view the hustle and bustle of London through the rain-streaked windows. "It's my first trip to London," she offered.

The driver glanced in his rearview mirror at a pert, dark-haired young woman in her early thirties. "Welcome, luv—I've been driving for thirty years—it's beginning to rack me nerves, it does." He pulled to the curb with a squeal of brakes. "Here we are, then." He stuck his arm out the driver's window and opened her door. She stepped out and paid him.

"Want me to wait, Miss?"

"No, I think I'll walk around after I get my rain gear."

He waved, "All right, then. Cheerio!" She watched the taxi weave expertly back out into the stream of traffic, the black car blending quickly into the flow.

Kate browsed through the covered Arcade and bought a suitable London raincoat and scarf, deciding the scarf could double as a hat. Leaving the Arcade, she turned up the collar of her new Burberry, looked across Bond Street, and spied the narrow side street and small antique shop the concierge had mentioned. Dodging between traffic, she arrived at the store, a quaint place with a potbellied bay window protruding out onto the sidewalk. Pushing the door open, she heard the tinkle of a small bell. Glancing up, she saw it was mounted on a curved piece of spring metal triggered when the door opened. The interior of the shop was warm and dry. There was a faint mustiness in the air. An elderly, grey-haired woman looked up from behind a cluttered counter, smiled and called out, "Good evening."

"Cool bell," replied Kate. "Don't see many of those today."

"Yes, I like the tinkling sound. I don't care for those horrid buzzer contraptions most shops use these days." She paused to push aside a pile of books and make space on the counter. "Had a chap come in and try to sell me one once, but I told him that bell had done its job for many years and I saw no sense going to a buzzer."

The shopkeeper had the bluest blue eyes Kate had ever seen. "I came in to browse around awhile," Kate offered.

"Good. Take off your raincoat." She indicated a large hall stand. "Give it time to dry out a bit."

Kate shrugged out of her coat, replying, "Thanks."

"No sense wandering around in a wet mackintosh. Best way to catch a cold. Besides, the hall stand needs some use."

Hanging up her coat, Kate noticed the stand was a single, beautifully carved piece of early Victorian rosewood. It reminded her of the one her grandparents had had in their home in Encino, California. The soft reddish-color wood was burnished to a glass-like finish from years of use and countless polishings. The attached mirror was unblemished, its edges beveled. In the reflection, she noticed a ceramic umbrella stand bristling with walking sticks and umbrellas. Walking over to it, she removed an umbrella with an elegant ivory handle, at once liking the feel. Standing straight, with the tip of the umbrella touching the floor, it was precisely the correct length for her. The smooth, curved ivory handle fit her grasp perfectly. Its soft cover fit flawlessly. She had to have it.

"Would you like me to open it for you?" the woman asked. "It's old, but there are no moth holes or anything like that. I furled it myself before adding it to the stand."

Kate fully trusted her word, and, thought that furled so neatly, it would take a monsoon before she would decide to unroll it.

"There is one unusual thing about it, though. Let me show you," the shopkeeper said. Coming out from behind the counter, Kate noticed she limped slightly. The woman took the umbrella, moved aside and pressed a cunningly hidden button where the handle joined the stem. There was a click, and a ten-inch steel blade leaped from the tip. "There, you see! Personal protection," she said, adding, "It's almost a sword."

"Isn't there a a law against that sort of thing," Kate exclaimed, eyeing the thin, gleaming blade warily.

"Oh, I don't know, it was made before the present laws; it belonged to a retired colonel from the Indian army. A fine piece of artistry and the inside of the stem has a thin sheath of lead to protect the steel blade from prying eyes."

"Thanks for showing me the hidden switch. I'd hate to have touched it accidentally walking through the park or someplace, and have the blade suddenly snap out."

"You're welcome, of course. Just hang it up there with your raincoat."

Kate gazed around; the place was crammed with odd and exciting articles, some hanging from the ceiling. Except for an occasional car horn as it passed down the narrow street, it was delishishly quiet. While she browsed, the owner returned to busying herself with old books and papers.

Kate was able to relax amongst the treasures scattered throughout the place. She had examined a couple of books and was replacing them back on a shelf when she noticed an old rocking horse half hidden in the shadow of a tall oaken bookcase. Moving closer, she noticed the paint had faded over time and a mane of dry, straggly gray hair sprouted from its neck. Its glass eyes glinted, the nostrils flared, and the lips curled, revealing a row of blackened teeth. She ran her hand over the saddle—real leather and well worn—as though a thousand children had straddled it over the years.

Kate tapped the frayed tail and the wooden steed rocked into motion with a slight creak and a steady even movement. It was an excellent horse. She placed her foot against the rocker, bringing it to a halt.

Suddenly the bell over the door jingled. A cold, wet breath of air swirled into the shop, and a man entered. He leaned back against the door, removed his cap and shook it out. He was tall, slim and in his late thirties. He removed the tan raincoat, stuffed his hat into one of the pockets, and hung his coat next to Kate's. Walking up to the counter, he spoke to the blue-eyed woman. While they talked, Kate moved to a section of old pottery and glassware. The man eventually left the counter, then walked to the rocking horse and began studying it carefully.

Kate continued inspecting various glass oddities, now and then glancing across toward him. She watched him as he nudged the horse, watched it rock with a critical eye and he slowly circle it like a judge at a horse show. Seemingly, he had not noticed Kate who had moved deeper into the shop and was standing in the shadow of a beautiful grandfather clock, watching him run his hands along the thin, timeworn leather reins and smooth its mane. He tilted his head from side to side scrutinizing the wooden charger. He seemed as taken with the rocking horse as had she.

Kate jumped when the Westminster chimes of the grandfather clock behind her tolled five times. The brass pendulum continued to swing silently, and Kate became aware of the soft tick-tock as the last of the chimes sounded through the shop, deep and melodious. The shopkeeper went to the front door and turned a hanging sign. It read, "open." Kate assumed the other side read "closed" and decided it was time to pay for the umbrella and be on her way. Moving past the never-ending assortment of clocks and watches, another sound came to her ears: a kettle whistling, shrill and urgent. She glanced back at the young man still standing beside the rocking horse and then at the shopkeeper.

"You will stay and have a cup of tea, won't you?" the shopkeeper asked, smiling as she busied herself with kettle and teapot.

"I lost track of time. I see you've closed up shop," Kate said.

"That's alright. I've plenty of tea. You should stay."

"Well, I don't know. I still have to pay for the umbrella," Kate took out her wallet and settled the bill.

"There; now you've paid. Now you really must stay for tea."

Kate hesitated. "I really should be going."

"Nonsense, besides the only thing out there at this time of the day is end-of-the-day traffic and rush—all push and noise." The shopkeeper suddenly stopped. "Oh, how silly of me. Perhaps you have an appointment?"

"No, I've no waiting appointment, just I didn't want to be a bother."

The shopkeeper's intense blue eyes sparkled. "Good." She indicated a couple of bentwood chairs behind the counter. "Sit down. There's nothing better than tea and toast when it's raining. Gives one a comfortable, secure feeling." She pointed to the window. "Just look out there." The rain had increased and was running down the windowpanes in rivulets, the street lamps amplifying the bleakness outside.

"I say," the shopkeeper called to the man, who turned with a surprised look. "Would you like a cup of tea? I'm closed now, and you can join us while we wait for the rain to slacken."

He hesitated for a moment, smiled, then walked toward them. "That's very nice of you. I'd love a cup."

"So now we're a trio," the woman stated. "Perhaps we should introduce ourselves. I'm Daphne Delferholm, the owner of everything you see around you. I live in the shop." Her brilliant eyes dulled for a few seconds. "My husband and I started the shop in 'thirty-nine, a few months before the war started. We lived through the blitz together until the night he was killed." Daphne gazed toward the front door. "He died right out there on the pavement. He was an air raid warden, you see, and was reporting for duty. The bomb landed close. Bond Street, in fact. He died from the blast. Never even cracked the window or a vase in the shop." She looked at Kate. "Don't worry, I'm not going to get maudlin—life's too brief for that. Being in antiques teaches one a good lesson of what life is all about. Life's a very short run for your money."

Kate and the male visitor arranged themselves on chairs behind the counter as Mrs. Delferholm opened a battered tea caddy and spooned out three heaping spoonfuls of black tea, glanced up and, adding a fourth, said, "And one for the pot." She poured the boiling water into the teapot then covered it with a woolen tea cozy. "We'll let it steep for a few minutes."

She sat down next to Kate. "Now, I've introduced myself. It's your turn." .

"My name is Kate Keenan. I'm visiting London for a few days. I live in Los Angeles, California."

Daphne nodded slowly and turned, offering her hand to the young man.

The man paused as if considering whether to take it or not and smiled. "Dan Blake. Just visiting."

"There we are, then: nice crisp introductions. Now that we know each other I'm going to call you Dan and you Kate; you must call me Daphne." She picked up the teapot, "Dan, milk, and sugar?"

"One sugar," he replied.

Daphne served Dan, then turned to Kate. "And you, Kate?"

"It's been so long since I had a real cup of tea, I'll go English style with milk and two sugars."

Daphne poured Kate's tea as two slices of toast creaked up from a battered toaster. "You'll find a plate under the counter, Kate. Butter them for me, will you? The butter is next to the biscuit tin."

Soon they were munching hot-buttered toast and sipping tea. Kate mentioned that the tea break was better than she could ever have imagined.

"Now this is what I call a pleasant end to a day," Daphne

said softly. "Better than pushing through the rush hour crowds in the rain, eh?"

The three exchanged glances and together agreed.

"I'm so glad you decided to stay. I don't get too many customers who have the same feelings you two obviously have for that old rocking horse."

Dan arched his eyebrows.

"Kate studied the horse at great length before you arrived, didn't you Kate?"

"Yes. I've always had a fascination for old rocking horses, and that one's a beauty."

"Anyone for more toast?" Daphne asked.

"No thanks, that was fine," Dan answered.

"Kate?"

Kate shook her head from side to side. "No, thanks."

"You know, I've had that rocking horse for years. Many people have looked at it. I very nearly sold it once to a couple from Bristol." Daphne sipped at her tea as she squinted at the horse in the shadows. "I purposely inflated the price, making it too high for them as I really didn't want them to have it." She caught Kate's eye and smiled. "You must think I'm a little dotty. Well, perhaps I am." Daphne tilted her cup and studied the tea leaves for a moment, then quickly placed her cup on its saucer.

"I almost forget the biscuits. Kate, please reach for the Crawford's tin under the counter and pass the biscuits around.

There are some rather good gingersnaps in there we can have with our second cup." Daphne commandeered the cups and poured again without asking. "Dip the gingersnap in your tea, Kate, but don't hold it for too long or it will melt and fall in."

"You know, this rather reminds me of the tea party in Lewis Carroll's *Alice in Wonderland*," Kate said.

Daphne nodded, agreeing. "Carroll's was a good tea party and a curious story. I must have read the book a dozen times when I was a young girl. I carried a first edition years ago."

The grandfather clock struck six. Kate was about to say she should be leaving when Daphne opened a silver cigarette case and offered it around, first to Dan who declined and then to Kate.

"No thanks," Kate said.

Daphne selected a cigarette and placed it in a long ivory holder colored dark ocher from years of use. Lighting up, she leaned back in her chair and blew a smoke ring. The three continued chatting awhile until, finally, Dan asked, "Well, Daphne, what do you think?"

"Fort Mead thinks highly of her," she replied.

Kate frowned. *Fort Mead? Part of the United States Intelligence and Security Command to whom she was initially detailed?* Who were these people? She hadn't even reported to DIA London yet.

Dan, seeing Kate's surprise, drawled, "Welcome to the

Three Brass Monkey's, Doctor Keenan."

A. G. Hayes

Chapter 4

Room 3388 at the British Ministry of Defense London is a poorly kept secret. Secretary Robert McNamara wanted it that way back in 1961 when he established a liaison office there under the control of the United States Defense Intelligence Agency.

A relatively small operation at first, its primary function was to represent the interests of DIA within the British Ministry of Defense, which, by custom, was called the "MoD." Over the years, DIA installed the usual array of modern electronic gadgetry, and supposedly, intrusion proof security. Nonetheless, it remained on the radar as far as MoD was concerned. "Something to do with the DIA" was as far as it went among the British spooks who inhabited the same building. Of course, everything was so obvious, no one would actually believe such rubbish.

Grainger Milburn, a grey-haired, pipe-smoking man well beyond retirement age, removed a pipe cleaner from the stem of his Birdseye Cavalcade Briar, blew into the stem a couple of times and eyed the man sitting across from him. He was looking at his replacement. Slowly he repacked the pipe bowl, relit and puffed a cloud of delightful-smelling tobacco across the desk. "The signal from Meade said you will be heading up the team investigating the Welsh affair."

"Yes, sir," replied Josh Rivet. Milburn had studied the man's dossier, and Rivet was a good replacement: an experienced man who had served through the rigors of Viet Nam as a lieutenant in command of a Riverine unit on the Mekong Delta. Battle-hardened, intelligent and politically perceptive of world affairs, he had to agree Rivet was the perfect choice.

"What are your feelings on working with an untested young woman posing as business magazine writer?"

"A problem, sir. I've read both her academic curriculum vitae and our dossier. She's not ready for this."

Milburn's pipe had gone out, and he automatically began going through the rituals pipe smokers do at this point, starting by knocking his pipe on the side of a cut glass ashtray on his desk. "Yes, perhaps. Nonetheless, Miss Keenan did well handling the mess from which she extracted herself in California. Her background in computer design will enable her to converse easily with the types we are interested in, and besides, she'll be working with Dan Blake." Milburn reloaded his pipe, lit up, tamped the tobacco with a seemingly fireproof index finger, and continued. "You know about the professor at her school in Switzerland I would guess?"

"Madam Zander?" replied Rivet.

"Yes. Madam Louise Zander." Milburn leaned back and looked at the ceiling through the smoke cloud. "I met her during the Cold War. Wonderful woman. We got her from the French after World War Two ended. She had been in the Marquis' and fought with the Free French. She finally left us and went back to teaching, ending up at an exclusive school in Switzerland."

"Yes. The Institute Surval Mont-Fleuri in Monteux, Switzerland," Rivet replied. "She'll be attending tomorrow's conference meeting and asked me to say she was looking forward to seeing you once again."

Milburn's eyes crinkled as he thought back to the past. "We can both look forward to meeting an extraordinary woman, Rivet."

A. G. Hayes

Chapter 5

At first, Kate wondered if this was a test by DIA to see how she would handle stress. The look in Dan's eyes, however, told her it was not. "Who are you?" she asked.

"Let's just say we're moonlighters, like you, currently working for the DIA."

Kate fumed—the whole damned thing was ridiculous—and tried to cover her anger by demanding to see their agency identification cards.

They were in order.

"Sorry for the deception, Kate," Dan said, "but we wanted to speak to you *before* you went to London HQ."

Kate remained indignant and anxious over the situation in which she found herself. "Did you follow me here, Dan, if that is indeed your name?"

"It is. I missed you at the hotel and tried to catch up to you at the Arcade. When I noticed you crossing Bond Street, I followed you here."

Daphne reached down and removed a small stone from inside her shoe, laid it on the counter, then removed her blue-colored contact lenses, set them beside the pebble, tearing and blinking rapidly.

Kate's eyes widened.

"That's right, Kate. Dan was supposed to greet you at your hotel and call me. When he didn't, I assumed he'd eventually catch up to you and bring you here. You're in a different world now, and Dan and I need to go over a few details before you meet the big guns."

Kate continued staring wide-eyed at the items on the counter and the remarkably younger-looking and sounding Daphne.

"Most people remember small things such as a limp," Dan murmured, "and blue eyes are also near the top of that list."

"So you two are the advance welcoming committee, is that it?"

Dan disregarded the sarcasm and continued. "I'll pick you up at your hotel in the morning. Then tomorrow, as planned, you will meet the right people, who, in turn, will welcome you aboard. Actually, it was your control at Meade who decided you should meet with us before going to London HQ tomorrow." Dan's voice turned deadly serious. "I hope that your background in computers and your journalistic cover will introduce you *entre nous* to many important business connections, in particular, Jones-Llewellyn Bionics in Wales. The British MoD—Ministry of Defense—is quite interested in one of their products, and at the same time, extremely touchy about it, hoping that no other country will learn of their radical advances in the world of artificial intelligence. If those radical advances are what they're said to be, that's sufficient reason for us having this chat before meeting tomorrow with Grainger Milburn and Josh Rivet."

Daphne picked up the conversation. "DIA London received word there's an ongoing disagreement between the principals of Jones and Llewellyn concerning the possible presence of a mole within their company. Llewellyn feels it a real likelihood. Jones argues that their company security is solid, but to ease his partner's mind, requested the UK government to run both an in- and outside-house security check. You're the outside expert chosen to certify the Jones-Llewellyn Bionics' situation."

Kate had been curious as to why DIA would become involved in what had seemed to her a clearcut case for British intelligence. Even more, why was she supposed to work with these two admitted "moonlighters?"

Dan, intuiting her unasked question, replied, "It was decided you should be accompanied by a couple of English agents to make it easier for you to be accepted here and to deflect any questions about your qualifications."

"Who exactly do you two represent, then, and what specifically are you bringing to this assignment?" Kate asked, looking from one to the other.

"Like you, we're both contracted to MoD. I was trained by the Vatican to represent the Church's interests in this matter, and I bring with that my extensive field experience working for both DIA and MoD. Daphne represents 'other interests', and brings with her more than an equal amount of field expertise, as you have seen." Dan pointed to the pebble and contact lenses.

Daphne nodded in confirmation.

"'Welcome to the Three Brass Monkeys'," Kate muttered. *An English agent with Vatican papers? An old appearing young woman representing 'other interests'?* she wondered. "What is he supposed to do, carry my iPad?" she asked Daphne.

Daphne smiled. "That can be arranged, if necessary. But for the moment, Dan needs get in touch with Zander before she meets with Milburn and the others tomorrow."

The name Zander rekindled a memory for Kate: Madam Louise Zander, an internationally known professor of applied economics. Then she remembered the last two lines of the phone message from MoD Control assigning her to London: "You will report to the London office and meet with someone you once knew when studying at the Institute Surval Mont-Fleuri."

Dan glanced at his wristwatch then dialed a number on his cell phone.

"I noticed the name Zander jogged your memory, Kate," Daphne said quietly. Dan, talking earnestly on his cell phone, had moved across the room next to the hall stand.

"Yes, though it's been awhile since I last heard that name. Will I meet her at tomorrow's meeting?"

Kate glanced at Dan, who nodded, recovered his coat and quietly left the shop.

"Perhaps this very evening," Daphne responded, leaving Kate to wonder why an elderly economics professor needed to be be present at a meeting of spooks. Her thoughts and the unusualness of tonight's meeting left her with a mounting anxiety. Her unease reminded her of a horrific situation two years ago in which she had had to fight a robot for her life. DIA alone was aware of the full story, and that Kate still suffered occasional flashbacks and nightmares over the episode.

A. G. Hayes

Chapter 6

Madam Louise Zander gazed thoughtfully through a filmy haze spiraling from the tip of her Galouse cigarette and took another sip of Courvoisier. Sitting alone in her hotel suite in London, she recalled what she had taught to so many of her young students over the years:

Applying economic theories to actual field conditions can be extremely helpful for two critical reasons:

First, applied economics sweeps aside any planned or unconscious attempts to dress up the situation so that it will appear to be worse or better than it actually is. From this perspective, applied economics is a powerful tool that enables a more accurate and complete picture to emerge, and makes it possible to rationally decide what to do and where to go next.

Second, applied economics provides a mechanism to determine the fundamental steps necessary to improve any current economic condition.

Louise sighed. Her words reminded that for years she had

hidden behind them, performing her duties faithfully in educating bright young minds, while nurturing a second agenda, one far more circumspect than economics. Louise was a "watcher," a person trained to see traits in a student that could lead to their enlistment in the field of espionage. Her phone rang, pulling her from her reverie back to the present. It was Dan. She affirmed she would be ready when he arrived.

Twenty minutes later, the doorbell jangled as Dan and Madam Zander entered the antique shop. Kate, still sitting next to Daphne behind the counter, recognized the woman at once. "Madam Zander," she said jumping to her feet.

"Kate Keenan," Louise Zander replied. "It has been a long time."

As they hugged, Kate became aware of the woman's thin, frail frame and the odor of tobacco surrounding her. Though noticeably older, her former teacher's eyes had retained their familiar determined glint.

Dan held a chair for her, and Louise sat down as if the walk from the front door to the counter had tired her. She unfastened the buttons on her long tan Burberry, lowered a battered leather briefcase to the floor, glanced at each of them in turn, then focused her attention on Kate. "I'm glad you decided to assist DIA in this mission, my dear. I gave them your name many years ago while you were still with us at the Institute.

"Why, Madam Zander?" Kate asked.

"Call me Louise; you're no longer a student. Besides being a teacher, I was—how can I put it?—a 'talent scout' of sorts."

Daphne was boiling water for more tea, and Dan pulled a chair up behind the counter, creating a semicircle, with Louise in the center.

"Did you recruit others while at Surval?" Kate asked, accepting the cup of tea Daphne had prepared for her.

"Oh yes, and it's still done in universities around the globe, in case you're wondering," Louise replied, looking wistfully at her tea after taking an exploratory sip. "You wouldn't happen to have some brandy, would you?"

Dan glanced at Daphne with raised eyebrows.

"There's a bottle upstairs in the kitchen cabinet," Daphne replied.

"Thank you for allowing an old woman an indulgence. I enjoy my tea the old-fashioned way whenever I can," Louise said. "Teaching economics is an ideal way to spot talent, Kate. The London School of Economics has an excellent record of recruiting; I must tell you more about that another day."

"Refill, Kate?" Daphne asked. "I made another full pot."

Kate hesitated, nonplussed. The last few hours in London seemed to make no sense. She felt as if she were in a stage play written by Agatha Christie, replete with pots of tea, chatty old women, antiques and rocking horses. Dan returned and poured a generous measure of brandy into Louise's teacup.

"Thank you, Dan," Louise said, then continued: "Kate, your expertise in computer sciences along with your DIA cover as a business magazine writer are instrumental to this operation. When we gather tomorrow morning, I guarantee the Brits will be recording every word."

"Then why meet at MoD?"

"We need them to hear *what we want them to*."

Kate shook her head in disbelief. Louise sounded like the Queen of Hearts in *Alice in Wonderland*. "By 'they' I take it you're referring to MI-6," she said, glancing at Dan.

"Yes. And the meeting in room 3388 tomorrow will include no mention of *our* interest in Jones-Llewellyn Bionics or what I'm about to tell you." Louise turned to Daphne. "Have you explained to Kate your part in the plan?"

Daphne shook her head in the negative. "Not yet, Louise."

"Then I think now would be a good time."

Daphne set down her cup and saucer. "Many years ago, I was an active spiritualist. Once or twice a week I would hold séances here in the evenings." She looked toward the rocking horse and smiled. "I told my clients that the horse was my channel, and in fact, it was, as far as I was concerned. All this was back before the war. My husband said it was all a silly game, but I didn't think so. By the late thirties, I had became reasonably well known, and it was during that time I met a Jesuit priest, Father Binchy, trained in Rome by Father Amorth in the art of exorcism. Father Binchy did not believe in my kind of spiritualism, of course. Nonetheless, we became good friends. In time, he informed me that the church was studying the possibility of alien life. Now, remember: This was over seventy-five years ago. The Vatican moves slowly and methodically. Few outside of the highest hierarchy knew of these studies until recently, when the Jesuit, Father Jose Funes, Director of the Vatican's Observatory, in a May 2016 interview in the Vatican daily, *L'Osservatore Romano*, was quoted as saying that believing in the possibility of the existence of extraterrestrial life was not opposed to Catholic doctrine." Daphne, her fingers tightly twined, paused and looked at the trio. "Father Binchy later told me it all comes down to faith. Faith was the shield with which one can readily overcome all evil."

"Ephesians Six: Sixteen," Dan appended.

For Kate, this conversation was getting increasingly weird; no more *Alice in Wonderland*, it was moving into something far more profound, far more *menacing* than DIA black ops.

Louise took over. "During the Cold War, Kate, intelligence agencies around the world made many concessions regarding whom they used, as well as how they used their unique talents. Daphne here became one of those people. However, as we know, with time, the human body and mind finally cease to run at peak efficiency, and as old age takes over, people are-prone to inventing things. At this time, it is global humanity that is slowly, imperceptibly inventing things, perhaps, as Father Binchy hinted, with a touch of the Satanic." Madam Zander took another sip of her 'toddie' before continuing. "I've something to read to you." She reached for her briefcase, placed it in her lap, opened the lid, removed a document stamped "EYES ONLY," and began to read aloud:

> After US deployment in two major theatres of war, the military have become keen to pursue alternatives to ground soldiers—'cannon fodder' as they used to be called—including Terminator-style armed robots. However, unforeseen issues have already arisen. A semi-autonomous robotic cannon deployed by the South African army in 2009 malfunctioned, killing nine friendly soldiers and wounding 14 others. To whom should we assign blame and punish for such improper conduct and clearly unauthorized harm? The designers, the manufacturer, the procurement officer, the field commander, the robot controller/supervisor, the head of military command, the leader of the country

or perhaps the robot itself? Patrick Lin, one of the authors of the report, emphasized that 'there are significant driving forces towards this trend.' In fact, the US Congress has already secretly mandated that by 2019, one-third of aerial vehicles, and by 2020 all ground vehicles need to be unmanned.

These deadlines apply immediate pressure towards the development and deployment of robots in military situations, while the rush to the market 'increases the risk of inadequate design or programming'. Recall Toyota's massive callback of automobiles in 2010 because of a computer malfunction in its computerized 'intelligent' braking system.

Louise stopped momentarily and peered at Kate over the top of her glasses. "There are those like this intelligence briefer but with significant field experience, who might say that computers work perfectly—until they decide not to. Right, Kate?" Louise slowly folded the papers and handed them to Kate, saying, "Read the rest of it at your leisure."

Madam Zander, Dan and Kate left the antique shop in true spook style, five minutes apart; Kate was second to leave. She took a cab back to her hotel. Despite or perhaps because of her jet lag and the gravity of the evening's meeting, it was well past midnight before she finally fell asleep.

A. G. Hayes

Chapter 7

A vivacious young female dressed in an oyster white blouse with navy blue blazer and black slacks crossed the sparsely furnished room. Her smooth gait reflected that of a trained dancer, though her work was far removed from that of a professional *artiste*. Terrwyn demurely slid into a visitor's chair facing a large oaken desk. Her hair, the color of toasted chestnut and worn shoulder length, gleamed with a healthy sheen. She was meeting with Doctor Eric Sykes for the first time; everything must go just right.

Three men observed her entrance through a one-way mirror. "Nice. Very nice indeed," murmured the senior partner of JLB—Jones-Llewellyn Bionics. The man's given name was Colgrevance. Tall, thin, aged fifty-six, Colgrevance Jones was known to friends and colleagues simply as Taff.

Taff turned toward his partner, Emlyn Llewellyn, shorter, stouter, aged fifty-four, who was standing beside him. The two had known each other since their student days at Aberystwyth

University while studying for their Ph.D.'s in Computer science and Cybernetics respectively.

"Yes, and the Ministry of Defense thinks so, too," grunted Emlyn.

The third person was Doctor Eric Sykes. Medium built, with piercing grey-green eyes, he was dressed casually in jeans and a tailored shirt. After observing the woman on the other side of the mirror for an additional few minutes, he ran a hand through a lustrous mop of brownish blond hair. "That is some good looking robot, Taff."

"Yeah, it is, isn't she? Come and I'll introduce you."

Terrwyn turned as the trio entered. Taff, arm outstretched, offered the promised introduction. "Terrwyn, Doctor Eric Sykes. Eric, this is Terrwyn. Her name is old Welsh. It means 'brave fair one'."

Terrwyn looked up at Sykes, her eyes glistening lively; there was no sign of the unnatural glazed stare of a typical cyborg. Terrwyn smiled, her breasts rising and falling gently as she seemingly breathed. and raised an outstretched hand toward him. "I am pleased to meet you, Doctor Sykes."

"The pleasure is all mine, I assure you, Terrwyn." He took her hand, finding it warm and natural.

"I heard you would be visiting from Yorkshire, and that you will be staying in Wales for a while," she replied.

Eric Sykes was not the kind of man easily impressed, but

what he was witnessing was far more than impressive: a robot with the ability to converse easily, and pass visually as a rational human being. This was the kind of proof he needed that all the time and money his company had invested into developing her organic digital brain, along with other humanizing talents built into Terrwyn, would pay off. No, it would do more than that. It would alter the course of civilization. Before he could speak further to her, Terrwyn rose from her chair.

"It was nice to meet you, Dr. Sykes; however, I must return to my quarters. We can, of course, talk further in the lab." Taff had purposively designed the initial proof-of-concept meeting to be brief.

Terrwin left, Emlyn following behind her.

Sykes watched their exit saying softly, "Terrwyn is the closest thing to a real human we've ever produced."

Dr. Eric Sykes, a universally renowned neuroscientist with an outgoing personality and boundless energy, had, after years of research and with the financial support of his company, Nano-Comp U.K., successfully created a working prototype of a human brain. His scientific team claimed that given time, they would build in sophisticated learning algorithms that would allow their creations to acquire and display appropriate human emotions as well as have the ability to think and learn on their own. Terrwyn was obviously the perfect showpiece.

Sykes, in a scientific paper a few months prior, had written, "It takes six people to operate a Predator Drone around the clock. The US Air Force has extensive computer software to train Predator operators. The day a computer can truly prepare a human for distance warfare, it can ultimately fly the drone itself." He was right and knew it. That's why he accepted Taff's invitation to visit. He wanted to see for himself what JLB had to offer in the way of robotics. Terrwyn was better than good. The thought of Taff's robotics using what he, Eric, now had waiting in the wings at Nano-Comp U.K. made him tingle.

For his part, Taff had issued his colleague the invitation hoping to impress Sykes into considering a merger with JLB.

On returning to Taff's office, Sykes crossed to a window and stared out toward Holyhead and the slate grey Irish Sea in the distance. "It's possible that by upgrading Terrwyn's neural network with our newest nanotechnology program I've designed, along with updates to her natural information processing, Terrwyn would be capable of independently processing information and making her own decisions. She would, in effect, be able to update and reprogram herself. Nano-Comp U.K. would bring her a step closer to perfection."

"An entirely free thinking robot! That's a tall promise, Eric," said Taff slowly.

Sykes, at first, didn't answer. His mind was far beyond

the horizon of the misty grey sea.

JLC was purposefully located several miles outside of Holyhead. Taff and Emlyn had planned a low profile operation located well away from prying eyes right from the beginning, having purchased an old deserted cotton farm perched on the slope of a rocky hillside. There they built their laboratory, by design keeping everything as near to the farm's original external appearance as possible. Many of the old stone outbuildings remained.

Sykes, and Taff, along with other like-minded scientists, were already becoming a concern to those in high governent places. For generations, powerful men and women had attempted to control the fates of nations; rumors of their successes and ultimate demise had come and gone, their memories eventually being relegated to the stuff of stories, myths and legends.

The twenty-first century had changed all that. These *Ubermensch* had always assumed their world to be populated solely by humans under their control; a place where the cleverest, fittest, most well-monied and powerful could rule and fool at leisure. Then, some in the Vatican had become uncomfortably aware of an approaching phenomenon soon to befall the earth: the realization that given the course of events, humankind could not be the *only* intelligent life form on the planet, and, in fact, never had been.

Sykes began to pace. "A tall order, maybe, but it *will* happen. We both appreciate the universal human need for a bridge between the old and the new, a fresh harbinger of a fresh realization and truth." What he didn't voice was his and Taff's secretly held conclusion like the Vatican's that eons ago another life force had existed that bore little semblance to humans today. Call it the "missing link," the human precursor or the progenitor that ultimately distinguished humans from other living forms.

Anthropologists and paleontologists had forever been announcing that the age of modern man—the Anthropocene Era, the period during which human activity was the dominant influence on climate and the environment—had come about with the arrival of Cro-Magnon humans in Europe. That was the "official" story. However, there was a slowly growing, implicit, universal suspicion that something was missing from this theory: namely, the *impetus* that was responsible for jump-starting the evolution of modern humanity. That a different life form, an extraterrestrial one—'aliens', if you will—had provided that jump-start was unheard of, and that there might be people today who still carried within their cells the genetic marker of this alien life force was, quite simply, unbelievable.

Sykes eyes narrowed. "You're referring, I assume, to the existence of a now repressed set of extra-human genes for intelligence?" *and the possibility of another set for intelligence in advance of our own*, he thought. How to explain a child prodigy who can play a piano concerto at the age of four, while most toddlers of the same age were typically destructive, unmanageable terrors? *One is blessed, the other possessed,* he thought. *Or vice versa.* He shrugged. "It is a part of our evolution that during this century we will discover that the ancient legends of Merlin, of wizards, witches, devils, and demons throughout the ages were, in fact, true, and that this genetic information remains part of us."

Taff grunted. "And you're referring, I take it, to your belief that the time will come when a computer, by being able to think for itself, will similarly spark within robots an age of intellectual, even spiritual evolution."

Eric nodded. "Yes, *especially* in robots."

Taff bristled. "As I said, Eric, that's a tall order and an even taller belief. Genes and traits have no part in either computers or robotics."

"Ah. Wait until you see Terrwyn fitted with my newest digital central nervous system and you'll better understand what I'm saying."

Taff's indignation cooled somewhat at the return of the thought of the merger. Sykes had indicated an interest in Terrwyn; the merger of the two companies would create an unbeatable force in the world of modern robotics.

Taff walked to his desk, sat down, and leaned back in his

swivel chair. If they were to become partners, it would benefit him to know everything he could about his potential partner's thinking. "Eric, when you mention genes and traits in the same breath as robots and computers, it leaves me more than a little confused."

Sykes lowered into a leather armchair on the other side of the desk. "How much do you know about the Vatican, Taff?"

Taff shrugged, "Not much, why?"

"They know all about people like you and me, and what we are doing with robots."

"How do you know that?" Taff squirmed uneasily.

"I make it my business to keep abreast of change. While the Vatican's power is waning, with over a billion adherents—three, if you consider the all different forms of Christianity as part and parcel of a Catholic—or universal—Christian Church, it still remains the most powerful organization directing human thought in today's world."

"You may worry over the Vatican, Eric, but I know that the Ministry of Defense is keeping a close eye on both of us. Everything from wiretaps to attempted cyber hacks…"

"What would be your reaction if I were to tell you that MI-5, MoD and any other security organizations you could mention are under control of the Vatican's own secret service?"

As a rule, Taff was an even-minded man who kept his own counsel as far as his business was concerned. But hearing such an outlandish statement from Sykes caused him to wonder if he had made the right choice in considering the man for a partner.

"I see by the look on your face," replied Sykes, "that you find what I've just said hard to believe, right?"

Taff started to speak, but Sykes held up his hand. "I agreed to visit, to check out your operation, see your product, and meet you in person." He paused, making a steeple of his fingers and rested his chin on the tip. "I like what I see, and that is why I am confiding in you. Do you want to know more? Or have you already decided to withdraw your as yet unspoken offer of a merger?"

Taff held up his hands in surprise. "I think Emlyn should also be present."

"I agree."

After Emlyn had walked Terrwyn back to her quarters— the Bio Vault—a modular unit providing a step-in environment located directly within the high security work place—she left Terrwyn and returned to her office. When she entered, the phone was ringing.

A. G. Hayes

Chapter 8

Kate ate breakfast in the hotel dining room. Two boiled eggs, wheat toast and a pot of tea. She didn't trust what remained of her jet lag hangover to anything more robust just yet. The meeting at room 3388 was scheduled for ten that morning, so she still had plenty of time. Yesterday's meeting with Daphne, Dan and Louise had left her wondering what today would bring. Finishing a second cup of tea, she became aware of the sound of her ring-tone, muffled and faint in the depths of her tote bag she'd placed beneath her chair. Retrieving it, she clicked the cellphone on and checked the screen for caller identification—there was none.

Reluctantly, she answered.

"Good morning, Kate. Sleep well?" She recognized Dan's voice. "Recovering from the jet lag?"

"Blackout, more like. I'm just finishing breakfast."

"Fine, I'll pick you up in five minutes." He hung up before she could answer.

Kate collected her tote bag, briefcase and umbrella and walked down to the lobby just as Dan entered. He looked refreshed and handsome in his Harris Tweed sports jacket, burgundy polo shirt, grey flannels and suede desert boots. He looked like an '80's actor going to audition for a part in a play.

Washed clean after last night's rain, London was a delight to behold as Dan drove his decrepit-looking Mini through rush hour traffic. "I felt it would be easier if we went in together. It's not an easy place to find." A red double-decker bus pulled out in front of them. Dan swerved hard right and squeezed between a motorcycle dispatch rider and another huge bus. Kate was petrified; Dan took it as a matter of course that came with driving in London's early morning rush hour traffic.

"Do we have far to go?" Kate asked.

"That's Whitehall. Over there. As I said it's not an easy place to find." He glanced in his side mirror. "Room 3388 that is. The MoD is an old monstrosity built in 1726 that adjoins British Army HQ. MoD used to be the Admiralty Building. Brits never give up their old buildings."

After parking and walking what seemed like a half mile, they entered a marble floor entrance hall and stopped before a wide staircase with a security desk on either side. The guards moved them as well as the rest of the morning crowd with practiced ease, and the two began their ascent. Four flights later, Dan indicated they should turn left down a shiny parquet floor corridor worn smooth and glossy from years of use. They had not spoken climbing the stairs. Despite that, Kate was short of breath when they stopped outside an unmarked door. Dan twisted the doorknob and pushed it open.

"After you," he said, indicating with an outstretched, upturned hand. They entered an oblong room with a number of people sitting along the sides in computer cubicles who ignored their entrance and just continued working.

As Dan shut the door, the door at the far end of the long room opened, and a tall square-jawed man with cropped ginger hair looked out. "Ah! Dan, come in, you're early." His sea green eyes scrutinized Kate as they neared. "The others will be along shortly. By the way, my name is Josh Rivet," His sea green eyes continued scrutinizing Kate. As she expected, Rivet's handshake was firm.

"Nice to meet you, Mr. Rivet."

"Josh, please. We keep on first name basis whenever possible. Glad to have you aboard, Kate. Just received a call from Madam Zander, her cab is being held up by a fender bender on Horse Guards Road."

Inside the room, Kate became aware of an aroma she had not smelled in years: Erinmore pipe tobacco, the tobacco her grandfather had smoked when she was child. Rivet pulled out a chair for Kate and they had no sooner seated themselves about a long mahogany conference table than the far door reopened, and a pipe-smoking man dressed in old tweed entered. Intuitively, Kate knew it must be Grainger Milburn, Chief of Station. He walked to the head of the table and adjusted himself into a battered leather swivel chair amid a cloud of blue tobacco smoke that swirled around his closely cropped greying head.

"Morning all. I see we are missing a couple of attendees." Josh brought him up to date on the delay of Madam Zander, and introduced her as Kate Pulaski, saying she was "on assignment" to ostensively interview leading British and European computer business CEO's on their feelings about the next business year's economy. From her meeting last night at the Three Brass Monkeys, Kate knew MI-5 would be listening to every word she said. It gave her an eerie feeling to know that DIA was running dis-information to the Brits on the Brit's own turf. Mindful of the report Madam Zander had read aloud in the antique shop and Kate had studied further that night, she wondered if the cover would be enough to satisfy MI-5 and her prospective interviewees in the job ahead of her.

Grainger Millburn's pipe had gone out, and he was scraping the bowl with some tool when the door reopened again. Madam Zander entered. Milburn set down his pipe and stood. "Nice to see you again Madam Zander. I know how busy you are."

As if pre-arranged, Josh Rivet took over the meeting.

"We'd like a few words on the state of the world economy and the time lag to global recovery. It might give Kate a few ideas for her interviews."

Madam Zander grimaced. "I'm sure Ms. Pulaski has already decided on her questions." She smiled graciously at Rivet, then Milburn. "No one knows for certain how long the recovery will take, seeing no one has the slightest idea how the economy went down like a house of cards in the first place." Madam Zander's voice was clear and steady as if she were lecturing at the London School of Economics.

Milburn puffed his pipe and remained silent.

"However, I have no doubt," she continued, "that there are those who *do* know and even knew how it was going to happen. Like the majority of economic failures in history, the answers typically come after those affected are dead, and the generation receiving the answers won't give a damn."

Kate guessed that was the signal for a change of topic. Madam Zander had given MI-5 enough upon which to chew. Rivet changed the conversation to a discussion on Trade magazine circulation numbers. The meeting droned on for almost an hour, and Kate was looking forward to getting out of room 3388. Rivet pushed a buff-colored envelope down the table toward Kate. "Here is the list of appointments your editor has arranged. Dan will go over them in detail with you later."

Milburn tapped his pipe on the edge of his chair and said,

"Well, it's time for lunch. I would like to invite the ladies to dine with me at Simpson's on the Strand. Josh and Dan have a lot of preparation work to do or I'd ask them to join us."

Kate hoped Simpson's on the Strand adhered to the no smoking law. Her jet lag momentarily reasserting itself, the idea of lunch with Milburn and his air pollution system was strongly off-putting.

They enjoyed a surprisingly pleasant lunch in the non-smoking restaurant. Milburn insisted they call him Grainger, and he entertained them with wild and wooly stories of his early days in the DIA, comparing them with the politically correct rubbish of today's intelligence services. Kate abruptly thought of her umbrella lying on the floor next to her tote and wondered what he would have said about it and its hidden blade.

They said their goodbyes at the entrance of the restaurant and thanked him. Kate wanted to get back to her hotel and read about the appointments DIA had arranged for her. Together, Madam Zander and Kate hailed a cab.

When Grainger Milburn returned to room 3388, he instructed Josh to take Dan to a pub lunch and update him about a man named Hank Tolomeo.

Dan considered himself an old hand in the espionage business; nevertheless, when Josh finished the story of Tolomeo, he was more than shocked.

"DIA *intentionally* placed Kate, untrained as she is, in harm's way?" he asked softly.

"Not unlike once before, Dan, and, unfortunately, it has to be that way, again."

"Surely they could have chosen someone specifically trained for this assignment. It's her first, for God's sake. She didn't even go through DIA Bolling," Dan argued, referring to Bolling Air Force Base Washington, DIA's training academy.

"With her experience and background in computer science, she was the best choice. The *only* choice. Her actions in the Bollywood case showed she could work under pressure. Besides she's not a career agent. Her relative innocence should help make her cover seem even more convincing."

"But being held hostage by one of Tolomeo's damn robots! It's no wonder everyone has been told not to mention his name in her presence."

"She showed the necessary presence of mind throughout the experience. It was the pivotal reason for choosing her for this assignment."

"And what happens if she finds out Tolomeo is working with or behind Jones-Llewellyn Bionics when she interviews Taff Jones?"

Josh took a last, long draught of beer. "She won't. Tolomeo is on the run. Besides, you'll be with Kate during all of her interviews to make certain that things like that don't happen."

"Who decided that and when?"

"Milburn cleared it with Mead and MI-5 an hour ago. You're to accompany Kate as her videographer, an acceptable arrangement in today's journalistic endeavors; it'll cause no suspicion and you'll be there to handle any untoward 'problems' that might arise."

"Does Kate know about this arrangement?"

"Not yet. When you go over her interview schedule with her, say that DIA decided she should have backup. You can add what you like to make it more believable, just don't mention the name Tolomeo."

Chapter 9

Eric Sykes leaned back in his deep-seated leather executive chair, his long legs stretching out toward a glowing log fire, sipping a glass of fine claret. "If the world is ready for a functioning robot secretary, for example, there is no need for a major technical breakthrough." He held his glass at eye level, twirled the stem and watched the flames of the fire reflect on the red contents. "A Tokyo subsidiary of 'Hello Kitty' maker, Sanrio Kokoro—which, by the way, means heart or mind in Japanese—is already producing advanced, talking, life-size humanoids. When questioned regarding their sense of 'presence', Yuko Yokota, Kokoro's planning department manager, stated emphatically, 'Robots have hearts. They can not look truly human unless we put souls into them. When manufacturing a robot, there comes a moment when a certain light glimmers in its eyes. That is when you know your work is approaching completion'."

Emlyn Llewellyn replied slowly. "She's right you know.

Absolutely right. I feel very much the same watching our creations 'awaken'."

Sykes changed the subject. "It's very kind of you to have invited me to your place for the weekend, Emlyn. I'm checked in at the lodge in Holyhead. I need to give them a call later to let them know where I am."

"I'm happy to have your company. Living alone is fine for doing my private research; but it does get lonely, and an occasional guest like yourself is most welcome."

"I would have thought you'd have enough of research at the lab every day."

Emlyn leaned forward and jabbed the logs with a long black poker causing a scattering of bright sparks to swirl up the chimney. "I never tire of my *private* research, Sykes," he clarified, and heaved another oak log into the glowing embers.

Emlyn's home stood in a peaceful location amid spectacular uninterrupted countryside with forest and mountain views. The original cottage dating back to to the early seventeenth century, it had recently been extended to provide visitors an inn-like experience with its extensive living accommodation. Located two miles from Pentraeth Beach, and reached via a footpath that meandered through the forest of Mynydd Llwydiarth, Emlyn Llewellyn' home was nonetheless within fifteen minutes of the A55 expressway and excellent road links along the North Wales coast into the seaport of

Holyhead.

A widower for five years, Emlyn lived alone with Max, his black Labrador Retriever. A local woman, Morgana Collins, came three times a week to clean and cook. Morgana was in her sixties, talkative and full of Welsh superstitions, which she passed on to Emlyn at every chance, including her staunch belief that the wizard Merlin was still alive and well.

Eric Sykes pulled his legs back from the blaze. "Can't argue with you there; the same's true of myself."

"Dinner's ready, Mr. Emlyn."

Sykes turned at the sound of the voice, to see a stout, red-faced woman in black standing in the doorway wearing a silver cross on a silver chain around her neck.

"Thank you, Morgana," said Emlyn, "We'll be right there," then to Sykes, "We'd better go in; she gets upset if her cooking gets cold."

The paneled dining room boasted a vast tapestry depicting hunting scenes hanging on one wall, and brass plates, two crossed Claymores and an eight-foot roundel of edged weaponry on the opposite. A dining table that could seat twelve with ease was set for two, with a candelabrum in the center holding four lighted candles. A discreetly placed floor lamp with several low-wattage lightbulbs glowed from within a fringed lampshade. Emlyn indicated Sykes chair. "I hope you enjoy Welsh rarebit, Doctor Sykes."

"I adore it, Doctor Llewellyn, second only to Yorkshire pudding." Both men were laughing as Morgana bustled into the room and solemnly set the food on the table.

They were at the cigar and brandy stage of the meal, when Emlyn stated, "I must tell you, Sykes: Taff was not happy when you mentioned your concern with the Vatican being generally against our research." Emlyn was referring to the meeting the three had had in Taff's office after their visit with Terrwyn.

"I would have been surprised if he hadn't," Sykes replied, blowing a smoke beam toward the ceiling. "All those Cardinals are like penned up foxes. One can never be sure what they are going to do next. Collectively, they appear to have no intention of aiding or abetting my work. In doing so, they broadcast to the world that they are against it and the world media reports that viewpoint."

"Sounds like something the Labor party would do," grumbled Emlyn.

Sykes grinned. "Exactly my friend."

Emlyn continued. "Taff is excited about recent tests carried out at the Bioengineering Department at Arizona State University. Preliminarly reports indicate that implanting arrays of electrodes into the cerebral cortex of monkeys allow them to record the electrical discharges of 50-80 individual brain cells, giving the most detailed and precise picture yet of how they communicate with each other. The signals intercepted by these electrodes are transmitted to a computer, 'decoded' and matched to different muscle movements. Another pioneering research group in Yorkshire is focusing its investigations on identifying the fundamental functions of the brain, which, as we know, is the single most complex organ in the known universe. They are working to create a hybrid organic-digital model in order to isolate, trace and document the functions of individual neurons, measure the various electrical interchanges, and download the information into a nanocircuit chip that can be inserted into a humanoid such as Terrwyn. By both internally and externally tracking changes in these neurons and analyzing them using an adaptive decoding algorithm, both the subject and the computer program 'learn' together. We're both at equally critical stages in our work, Sykes."

"You're right, of course," Sykes agreed, "A shared, interdisciplinary approach is what's needed to open the door to allow artificially intelligent humanoids to evolve like we humans have, but with assistance of advanced nanocomputer technology, making their progress, hopefully, a damn sight faster."

"What new thoughts will come to such humanoids? Will they soon think in such a way that we will no longer be able to understand their thoughts and reasoning?" Emlyn sighed. "I wish Taff were here to be part of this conversation."

Sykes said nothing, but nodded his agreement and continued sipping his drink.

Chapter 10

Sykes shaved, showered, and went down to join Emlyn for breakfast before he became fully aware of how silent the house seemed. Crossing the hall, he entered the dining room and found the thick brocade entrance curtains still drawn. Moving down the hallway, he checked the study. No one there. While wondering if maybe he was simply too early for Emlyn, he suddenly realized the stillness was total. There was no one at all in the house. To be sure, he went to the kitchen. Morgana had asked him how he liked his breakfast eggs last night before he'd retired. The kitchen was empty. *It might be Morgana's day off, and Emlyn may have gone for an early morning walk,* he told himself, checking his watch. It was almost eight o'clock in the morning.

He made toast and was having a second cup of tea when the telephone in the hall jangled. He picked up but only heard a dial tone. An old style phone, he jiggled the receiver bar, but, unable to establish a connection, hung up and stared at the phone. He walked to the front door and found it unlocked. Perhaps Emlyn had forgotten about the breakfast arrangements and gone for a walk with his dog, and, being a proberbial absent-minded professor, Emlyn was somewhere about the grounds.

By nine-thirty, after walking the paths of vast gardens that seemed to go for miles surrounding the house, Sykes decided something was wrong. Having forgotten to bring his cell phone, he returned to the house where he dialed the UK number for emergency—999.

The following hours were frenetic: Local police arrived within the hour, quickly followed by MI-5. Minutes later the army was searching the hills, woods and countryside around Emlyn's home.

When questioned at her home, Morgana told the police she had received a call early that morning from Emlyn advising her that he had changed his mind about breakfast. He said he and Sykes would be going into town for breakfast, so she wouldn't be needed until evening. The police checked phone records and verified Morgana had received a call at six-thirty that morning from Emlyn's home number. Sykes spent hours answering the police and MI-5's seemingly endless questions. It was as if Emlyn had vanished from the face of the earth.

Chapter 11

When Jilly Suede heard that Hank Tolomeo, the man from Kate's past whose name MoD had reminded Dan Blake to strictly avoid mentioning, had up and left London for Wales, she didn't think to miss Hank at all. Jilly needed time to herself after months of being a fugitive on the run with Tolomeo, hiding in one country after another. Tolomeo had finally taken Jilly's suggestion and sold the damn yacht they'd used to escape the United States and that they'd left in Mexico, and the two had headed for Europe. The upside of escaping justice was they'd come out with most of the tens of millions of dollars they'd made from their work together in the USA over the last decade.

Jilly scanned the fresh pile of dark green boxes containing purchases from Harrods stacked on the floor of their posh London hotel. She loved London, and she loved to shop. Nonetheless, they were both fanatically aware it was essential that they maintain a low profile—likely *forever*. They would buy a country home in Wales if Hank decided it prudent to invest with his old acquaintance, Taff Jones. That way they could buzz up to London now and then as other well-off couples do. It was almost five o'clock in the evening. Jilly went to the drinks cabinet, poured herself a tall glass of champagne and wondered briefly what the poor people of the world were doing.

"No one must know I'm in Wales, Taff," Tolomeo said, sitting in Taff's study in the man's home outside of Holyhead. Tolomeo's egotistical bent, which he'd developed in early childhood, a characteristic that had made him a fabulously wealthy bastard, called for him to be forever in charge. However, like so many others of his ilk, greed quickly overtook common sense.

Tolomeo had known Taff for years through a mutual interest in the manufacturing of electronics and robotics. He had first contacted Taff from California and informed him of his decision to sell his company, Tolomeo Technics shortly before his disastrous interaction with Bollywood movie Mongol, Kumar Pashagora. Together, they had unsuccessfully attempted to acquire some advanced cinematic technology from a then unknown programmer, Kate Keenan. Up to this moment, Taff, like many of Tolomeo's former associates, believed he and his fiancé; Jilly Suede, had perished at sea in their yacht.

"Your secret is safe with me, Hank," Taff said, topping up Tolomeo's glass with a splash of Black Label. "Damn glad you kept your Christian name when you and Jilly changed identities. I've known you as Hank for so long, it would've been too easy to slip up."

"Yeah, I employed the best frigging forger there is in the identity business. He worked for the United States' Federal Government, then found out he could earn more freelancing than designing new documents for the Witness Protection Program. He said always stick as close as you can to the truth and keep your original Christian name. It makes lying easier. So, Jilly and I did."

"Wise advise, Hank."

Hank sipped at his scotch. "Jilly and I have a new last name: Fannon. We're Hank and Jilly Fannon now. So it's your turn: Tell me about Eric Sykes. I know he's one smart neuroscientist. I know of him from his work with Henry Markham on the Blue Brain Initiative to create a working, digital version of the human brain by reverse-engineering mammalian brain circuitry. That was back in 2005. Why would he want to merge with Jones-Llewellyn?"

"Simple: He's been busy making functional digital brains that mimic human brains, while I've been busy making functional robotic bodies that mimic the human body. If we were to pool our talents, who knows what would result?"

"So where do I fit into this interesting dynamic?" Hank held up his glass for a refill.

"You were on a first name basis with the top people in the business of robot design and manufacturing all over the world. You hold many interesting patents for which Ishikawa Metrics and others, like JLB, would gladly pay your estate millions to own," Taff said as he poured more whiskey. "If we could agree to work together, I'm willing, in addition, to offer you alongside Sykes each a third of the final profits when Terrwyn is fully operational as an independent decision-making humanoid."

Both were aware that the robotics industry had made significant, though less well known strides outside of manufacturing and automotive industries. Various types of robots were even now being designed for use in demolition, surgery and war as well as for air, underwater and domestic operations. The Japan Robot Association estimated that the Japanese robot industry would be worth approximately $28 billion by 2015, and $75 billion by 2021. The service robot industry was no longer something coming—it was here today.

Hank's gut feeling told him Taff was not offering a third of his business simply to garner his goodwill and the patents JLB was vying with Ishikawa Metrics to obtain. "My connections and patents for a third of the company?"

"There are a couple of details I'd need to add to the pot."

Hank grunted. "Such as?"

"Well, Sykes and I are primarily researchers—doctors of science—and increasingly out of touch with the everyday business world. Too much time spent in the lab, with business being a completely different world these days, eh? You, on the other hand, have the knowledge and the ability to do 'effective business' as well as contact and—how shall I put it?—'enjoin' people of particular interest to us. The British government is extremely interested in my work and is already busy trying to make sure it does not fall into 'the wrong hands', some of which, if under our control, could prove immensely helpful to our effort and lucrative to ourselves."

Hank Tolomeo, now Hank Fannon rose, walked across the room, and stood with his back to the open fireplace, rubbing his buttocks in the heat from the log fire, staring at the ceiling. After a few moments, he said. "The government will eventually try to get involved and sequester your work. That in iteself can be quite lucrative, though, from a researcher's point of view, unacceptably restrictive. All this makes me think that you already have a plan of your own. Taff, you sly bastard, are you wanting me to arrange a 'robot robbery' and make Jones-Llewellyn look like the victim?" Hank swigged the last of his drink. "If so, you've definitely been in the lab too long. If the government's involved, then MI-5 would also be, and MI-5 would see through that old chestnut right away."

"Not if the robbery had 'political overtones'," Taff said softly. "You have international connections. Like with India."

Hank eyed Taff over the rim of his glass. "You mean Pashagora? Wise up, Hank, that guy's really bad news. If he ever finds where I am right now, I vanish and JLB likely would, too."

"That's ridiculous," Taff, sputtered. "The government would never allow it to happen. Besides, our security is top of the line."

"From what I hear, it didn't help Emlyn much."

"Emlyn was at home."

"Just like you are right now. No, Taff, Pashagora is out of the question. But..."

Chapter 12

Kate checked the listed appointments Josh Rivet, her liaison with MI-5, had given her at the meeting, noting the interviews all were with scientific types: two, three, even four a day depending on the travel time between sessions. She glanced up at the sound of a knock on her hotel room door.

"Who is it?"

"Dan. Let me in."

Kate opened the door and Dan pushed his way in looking agitated. "Are you all right?" she asked.

"Not really. Traffic jam and a two-mile tailback."

"You look like you need something to drink. Sit."

"That's not all; Doctor Emlyn Llewellyn of JLB, one of the most important persons on your list, has gone missing. Vanished. No one knows what happened. Soda's fine."

Kate grabbed a couple of Cokes from the fridge. When she returned, Dan was reading over her appointment list, and looked up. "Looks like a lot of work. Unfortunately, we may not be able to get near JLB with Doctor Llewellyn missing."

"When did this happen?" Kate asked.

"All we know at the moment is Doctor Emlyn Llewellyn has not been heard from since he had dinner with a colleague, Doctor Eric Sykes, last night."

She handed him a soda. "What did Josh mean when he said you would be going with me?"

Dan slumped into an armchair after taking a long swallow of Coke.

"Well, for one thing, I'll be going with you."

Kate frowned. "Since when?"

"Milburn told Josh I was to go as your videographer. As a 'government man', it'll make your visit appear officially sanctioned—a safety measure, especially if security is tightened. Given the situation, the lab may end up being closed to outside visitors."

"This is my first assignment, and it already feels more like a practice run through a lunatic asylum; it's no wonder espionage personnel are a different breed. A spiritualist/exorcist who runs an antique shop and uses a rocking horse to channel to another world? And Madam Zander should have been retired years ago, but is still working with DIA. In the meantime, I'm assigned to sniff around robotics labs to see what I can find out, while the government is dead set that no one will find out anything about all this. I'm a trained scientist, educated to do everything 'by the book', one line at a time and get it right. Now, unless you can spell out my assignment in clear, understandable terms and give me a clear, understandable reason for your tagging along, I'm ready to quit and return to computer research."

Dan squirmed deeper into the chair. "Look, that's only part of it. There's more: The document Madame Zander read to you at the Three Brass Monkey's is true. A significant part of the new arms race involves robotics; especially designs that do not look like what most people think a robot should. The Brits want nothing to slow down the JLB effort." Dan rubbed a hand through his hair, hesitated, then continued. "I could be fired, maybe locked away for what I'm about to tell you."

Kate moved to a chair opposite him and perched on the edge of the seat.

"My most recent employer, the Vatican, is also involved, Kate, and I want you to listen carefully to what I'm about to say. Before you joined DIA, you had became a pawn in a game that has already once almost cost you your life. The US government noted your determination and logical thinking and more so, the quasi-governmental agency, Cerebrus, for whom you currently work. Throughout your nightmare, two people were intent on seeing you dead: Hank Tolomeo and Jilly Suede."

Kate's heart thumped at the mention of the names.

"The story was they both perished at sea on their yacht attempting to flee the USA. But they didn't die, Kate. Hank Tolomeo and Jilly Suede are in the UK right now, and Jones-Llewellyn Bionics, who is in the last stages of manufacturing a robot with the ability to pass as a thinking human being, is in the process of making a deal with Tolomeo."

Dan watched the color in Kate's face drain and raised a hand to stop her from speaking. "Milburn left you out of the 'need to know' loop. I've decided, however, that given the situation, you *need to know everything*.

"The Vatican has historically been dedicated to saving human souls, and exploring what it means to have one. Recent research suggests it is only a matter of time before the human race learns that, as an increasing number of ancient documents infer, we were not the first of our kind, but a continuum of a race that once lived on this planet. This is so momentous a discovery that it is only a matter of time before it leaks out, and the Vatican wants to be fully prepared for the upheaval it will cause within the church. Due to the growing popularity of the Internet, there have already been hints, and scholarly articles have appeared indirectly discussing the possibility of the truth coming to light. A corollary is whether *our* souls are the same as those of the original race—a hot topic at the moment—and whether humanoid robots indistinguishable from us—ones like Jones-Llewellyn Bionics are about to unveil—have or will somehow acquire souls."

"The Vatican is getting prepared to publicly admit all this?" Kate asked softly.

"No, of course not," Dan answered quickly. Kate was the sort of person who could walk into a new country in the morning and throw away the need for a map at bedtime. Bringing her into the loop would vastly increase their likelihood of success even though he had no authorization to reveal what he had thus far revealed or more.

"I have come to believe there are those who are a tad different than most of us walking the Earth. The Vatican firmly believes this, and so do DIA and most intelligence agencies around the world," he offered obliquely.

"Wait a minute," she said. "The Vatican, the international intelligence services, robots, other species who perhaps have existed longer than we have—who's controlling *them*, Darth Vader?"

Dan reached into an inside pocket of his jacket and removed an envelope. "This may help begin to answer your question." He selected a page and began to read aloud: "The actions by the Vatican and the U.K. Ministry of Defense have become so closely coordinated in time—often separated by less than twenty-four hours—that it seems not unreasonable that the Vatican Intelligence Agency (SIV) and the British MoD are more than synchronistically linked." He looked up to see if what he was reading was fully registering. Satisfied, he continued. "It increasingly appears that they represent the first two parts of a new, global intelligence arrangement being established amongst the world's intelligence services."

Dan folded the paper. "That's a memo we, the Vatican, intercepted two days ago. Now I can fill you in on what we know to date."

"So you're an Englishman working for *at least* three intelligence services. Okay, but before you go on, tell me one thing."

"Sure."

"Why can't someone in this 'new, global' association of interrelating intelligence services simply remove Hank Tolomeo from all this?"

"He holds multiple citizenships, British and American being the most obvious two. His mother was British, and Hank Tolomeo, being born in America, legally claimed dual naturalized citizenship in the UK. In addition, his former company interests place him in the enviable position of being a person-of-interest to multiple governments, all quite willing to grant him additional citizenships and other governmental advantages in hopes of enticing him to share his expertise in robotics with them. In fact, he carries numerous passports, some legal, others not so legal, making establishment of jurisdiction a quagmire.

"What about Jilly Suede?"

"Technically, she and Tolomeo are living in London under the family name 'Fannon'. My orders are to not bother her, and thereby not spook Tolomeo."

Kate had secretly harbored the ugly suspicion that Tolomeo and Suede were still alive, and now a huge surge of adrenalin seized her. She could be instrumental in catching those bastards and bringing them to justice. "You and DIA have just made my day, Dan; I can hardly wait to nail that swine, Tolomeo. I'm armed, trained, and have a license to kill."

Her outburst of enthusiasm was the last thing he had expected. "Whoa! Hold it Kate; there's more: The robots Tolomeo has an interest in have a technical problem: They had to be made sophisticated enough to fool us into thinking they were human. As a result, they have already learned how to override their programming and ignore commands given to them. No one knows how, or whether this new ability is an indication of something greater. Their self-reprogramming has resulted in their programs becoming so complex, their creators can no longer read or understand them."

That got Kate's attention. In her last year at UCLA, she had heard vague reports of such phenomena: computers teaching themselves how to learn; 'doing their own thing'. Some said it began with a virus. There were others of the school of technological singularity, who stated that machines when complex enough would reach a level *par excellence* with humans, and the occasional blips and another odd phenomena that often appeared were subtle signs of their advancement. They reflected the thinking machine's ability to start, process and stop on its own. Kate had all but forgotten about the heated discussions on this topic and eventually relegated them to just another collegiate gossip. Hearing it again from Dan, along with Madam Zander's reminder that a semi-autonomous robotic canon deployed by the South African army "malfunctioned" in 2009, killing nine friendly soldiers and wounding fourteen others, put things in a different light.

"Kate, Tolomeo is a 'Golden Boy' as far as MI-5 is concerned. They want nothing to happen to him until Jones-Llewellyn Bionics have their wonder robot fully operational and in production. Remember, the British government wants an exclusive on this. No other countries, including the US, are to even get a look at the product or prototype. Everyone in the US, of course, but you."

"Publicly, the British don't seem very concerned about rogue robots," Kate snorted. "And I personally know Tolomeo as a money-grubbing…"

"Kate. His parent company in California had extensive connections. Aside from his experience in robotics, TolomeoTechnics spent months researching the use of miniature nanoparticle smart 'bombs' to defragment errant code on the hard drives of his various robots. In the end, it did no good, of course. But in the process he became aware it was only a matter of time before 'thinking machines' would learn to use this kind of technology to program and advance themselves. He even had a name for it: "Intelligent, Nascient, Self-Directed AI Nanotech Evolution"

"It makes for an interesting acronym: INSANE," Kate mused.

Satisfied Kate had a better understanding of the situation facing her, Dan switched the conversation back to the government's security forces, reminding her they would be following their every move and word. Together, they would have to carefully evade the very people to whom they'd been detailed, and relinquish any notion of extracting revenge for everything Tolomeo had done to Kate. "Look. Today's schedule is off while authorities try to find Dr. Llewellyn. I'll be back in the morning. Breakfast at eight-thirty sharp, then we start out for Holyhead. The rest of what I have to tell you will take up the entire time we'll spend driving there."

A. G. Hayes

Chapter 13

No one at JLB could believe such a thing could happen. Twenty-four-hour, seven day-a-week uninterrupted top-of-the-line security, and Emlyn had vanished from his own home. A doleful assembly listened to Doctor Taff Jones' abbreviated announcement about Emlyn's disappearance at a meeting in JLB's main laboratory. Among those present was Dr. Gwyneth Evans, a close colleague of Llewellyn and second in command of security. As scientists and lab workers filed from the meeting, Taff called Gwyneth aside and said, "We must carry on, Gwen, and hope for the best. Emlyn would want it that way."

"Will Nano-Comp still be merging with the company?"

"Oh, yes, Gwen," Taff replied in earnest, as they exited the meeting room together.

The next morning, Dan arrived at Kate's hotel in time for breakfast as promised.

"Pack for a couple days," he advised while buttering the

toast. Kate looked significantly less enthusiastic than the day before. Dan frowned. "You okay?"

"Physically I'm fine; it's just unnerving knowing Tolomeo and Suede are so close and I can't do anything at all."

Dan pushed the marmalade toward her. "Don't fret. Try some of this. We limeys make the best marmalade in the world."

Undeterred by Dan's flippant remark, Kate continued: "How long is the drive to Holyhead?"

"We should be there by evening."

"Does MI-5 know about the Three Brass Monkeys?"

They've knew about it a few hours after DIA moved in with them, and that was in 1961. There's not much they don't know; we simply need to keep them from knowing too much."

Kate tried the marmalade. Dan was right; it was particularly good. "Knowing too much about what?"

"That you and Tolomeo, for instance, have a particularly complex history."

Kate ignored the remark, assuming from what he'd said previously that MI-5 would know fully well all about that. Dan was clearly avoiding answering.

"Was Daphne doing her séances in 1961?" Kate asked, changing the subject.

Dan shrugged. "I never asked. Why?"

"Just wondering. If, as you said, MI-5 knows about the

Three Brass Monkeys, then why bother keeping the place?"

Dan smiled. "So MI-5 can leak disinformation to other agencies through us."

Kate drained her teacup. "I'll get my bag and be right back."

"I'll be waiting in the lobby."

She returned few minutes later, pulling a single small-wheeled luggage, her umbrella tucked neatly under arm. Dan was sitting in the lobby reading the *London Times*, and seeing her, glanced up. "I'm impressed. Most women take an age to pack."

"I packed most of my things last night. And, for the record, I'm not like 'most other women'. Now let's get going, I want to learn more about the Vatican's distress over humans having a previously unknown history no one until recently ever suspected, and all you know about human-made egotistical robots."

A. G. Hayes

Chapter 14

Despite being chosen to replace Grainger Milburn, Josh Rivet was not a happy man. Taking over the position meant he would be inheriting a number of complicated situations. He was already responsible for the Welsh affair, and that damned woman posing as a business reporter sent over to snoop around could screw up everything. He had assured Dan that Kate would never meet up with Hank Tolomeo; nonetheless, given the evolving situation, it could very well happen. And Kate Keenan was not the biggest of the problems that demanded his immediate attention. Sighing, he reached for his phone and called an old and trusted MI-5 field colleague, Jack Drummond.

They met at the Café in the Crypt at St Martins in the Fields Church in Trafalgar Square, Drummond joining Rivet who had been sitting patiently at a table beneath the vaulted brick ceiling towering over the historic gravestones lining the crypt floor. The two quietly surveyed the menu.

"I never thought of you as a church-going man, Josh," Drummond commented, after the waiter left with their orders.

"You're right; nonetheless the Crypt serves the best treacle pudding in London."

"You didn't ask me here just to eat treacle pudding together, I hope."

"Of course not. The fact is, we have a collective problem —an impending crisis actually—and it concerns the Welsh affair."

"Do tell."

"Kate Keenan, newly detailed help posing as a reporter for a business magazine, is scheduled to visit Jones-Llewellyn Bionics and interview Taff Jones."

"That's not exactly a crisis, Josh. She won't be allowed to see anything she shouldn't. Internal security there is tight."

"What does the name Hank Tolomeo mean to you, Jack?"

"Nothing much. Should it?" Both men fell silent while the waiter served their lunches.

When the waiter left, Josh resumed. "Then it's time I filled you in."

Drummond listened attentively as he ate and Josh brought him up to date.

Before Jack was halfway through his chicken, he placed his silverware down and frowned. "Nothing must interfere with the completion of the Jones-Llewellyn project," Drummond said with cold finality. "Call her temporarily back. We'll find Tolomeo and the Suede woman, and this time they'll really disappear." Drummond pushed back his chair. "I've got to get my people on this immediately. I'll take a rain check on the treacle pudding."

Josh finished his lunch alone, glancing at his watch while he waited for dessert.

On the way to his car, Drummond contacted Thames House and spoke to Head of Security Service MI-5 who, already aware of the growing situation, suggested that Kate and others might have been bugged by one of Tolomeo's many confederates long ago. Assuming so, Drummond would have to locate Tolomeo and Suede the old-fashioned way.

Dan wove through London and into the countryside, heading toward the A5 Motorway that would take him and Kate Keenan to Wales. When the Mini-Cooper began clicking off the motorway miles, Dan said, "Ready for your lesson in apolitical management, Kate?"

"Yes."

"Okay. The Vatican's interest in an extraterrestrial presence goes back a long time. Exactly how long, we do not know, so we will start with Pope Benedict the Fourteenth, and the Jesuits and Vatican Intelligence Agencies of that time. An interview with Reverend Jose Gabriel Funes, the Jesuit director of the Vatican Observatory appeared in the official Vatican newspaper, *L'Osservatore Romano* on May 13, 2008, on the ninety-first anniversary of the Fatima miracle of May 13, 1917. The interview was meant to be supportive while preserving plausible deniability: however, Funes was quoted as stating that the existence of extraterrestrials didn't contradict the Catholic faith because aliens would still be God's creatures." Dan increased his speed to overtake a lumbering furniture truck.

"I thought that kind of story belonged on the social internet alongside flying saucers and little green men."

"I've not finished. During my training, I was directed to attend a special seminar in room 3388, and believe me it was the most informative seminar I ever attended. Anyway, prior to that, an informal apolitical representative of the Vatican, Monsignor. Conrado Balducci, had delivered a keynote speech at the 2005 X Conference in Washington DC in which he mentioned similar doctoral highlights which also intimated a shift in Vatican theology to include extraterrestrials as part of God's creation, which, when later restated by Reverend Funes in *L'Osservatore Romano*, made it official."

"Just what is 'apolitical management' and what does it imply? Remember, I wasn't at your seminar meeting."

"Do you enjoy dancing, Kate? Because from now on, we are going to be dancing with the devil. Inbetween lines, Baldacci's keynote speech suggested that sophisticated electronic devices, including computers—especially robots—

could be susceptible to the same extraterrestrial presence as our current human race."

As Chief Scientist for Cerebrus, Kate had 'danced with the devil' a number of times before at blue sky meetings where scientists and engineers allowed their imaginations to run wild. Hearing what Dan was telling her and well-understanding what the name Tolomeo meant in the realm of commercial robotics was pushing her to the edge of reality.

Returning to her original question, Dan explained that 'apolitical management' was an inside way within the Vatican to refer to the Church's new recognition of the science of outer space. It was the science of relations between our human civilization and previous, current and future advanced civilizations throughout the universe. "The United Press used the word 'exopolitics' and saw it nominated for two-thousand-five's New Word of the Year. Such words and concepts may be new to the world, but not to the Vatican," Dan explained. "For example, during my training, I learned that Cardinal James Francis Macintyre of Los Angeles, had been chosen by then USA President Dwight Eisenhower as a 'cultural witness' to his secret meeting with a purported group of Nordic Extraterrestrial Ambassadors at Murdoc Dry Lake Army Air Corps Base in California on twenty through twenty-one February nineteen fifty-four. Today it's known as Edwards Air Force Base. The Cardinal flew to Rome to brief the Vatican after the Eisenhower meetings. You know the old saying, 'politics make strange bedfellows'? Well, in this day and age it is taking on a different connotation altogether."

"Thanks for the informative lecture," Kate muttered, wondering if this was a further test of her objectivity or sanity. Her concern was enhanced by being incensed that Tolomeo and Suede were living in the UK—and no one back home either knew about it or, if they did, intended to do anything about it. "Dan, I know this briefing is meant to help keep me on track and save my ass with the DIA, but…"

Dan cut her off in mid-sentence. "I know you're new to what must seem a truly bizarre mind-game rife with aliens, souls and subterfuge, but the bottom line is, we live by orders or leave the club. I'm briefing you against my own orders because sometimes I have to follow a hunch." The dash clock showed it was past noon. "Let's stop for a reality check: a good pub lunch. We're already in Warwickshire. Atherstone is a few miles ahead, and there's a pub there I like called the Ferret Tavern.

Feeling equal parts disoriented, frustrated and hungry, the idea of a pub lunch seemed an excellent suggestion to Kate. Fifteen minutes later, they drove into the parking lot of the tavern. The pub proved charming: beamed ceilings, an open fireplace and a welcoming atmosphere oozing palpably from its ancient walls.

Dan suggested a pint of the house's best bitter as they found a table near the bar. Kate agreed to a half pint. The chalkboard menu on the wall listed a range of strange-sounding foods. Dan recommended a Ploughman's Lunch, explaining it consisted of crunchy bread, cheese, tomatoes, and lettuce, plus a couple of pickled onions, the cheese and pickles coming on the side. With her agreement, he went to the bar, placed the order, paid and returned with the two beers.

Kate sipped lightly at her half pint. "I'm not much a beer drinker, Dan, and this is…so different from America. Even the beer."

Dan downed half of his before speaking. "That's real beer you have in your mug, Kate, not American fizz water."

The Ploughman's Lunches arrived, each on an enormous plate. Four chunks of cheese—mature cheddar, some Stilton, a thick slice of ripe Brie, and a contrasting Double Gloucester—with a fresh, home-baked, crusty French roll, a Bramston Pickle, two pickled onions, a field tomato and a hard-boiled egg on the side. Kate immediately saw the logic to separating the cheese and pickled onions. If pre-placed on the bread, one wouldn't be able to open his or her mouth wide enough to eat it.

Kate thoroughly enjoyed the break, and when they had finished, felt more like herself. Reaching for her purse, she took out a roll of mints and offered one to Dan. He laughed and declined saying he wanted the taste of the lunch to remain with him a while. She opened her purse to replaced the roll of mints and noticed a paper napkin folded neatly at the bottom of her bag—then remembered; she had bitten down on what looked like an uncooked grain of rice while eating dinner on the plane. She had folded it into her napkin intending to mention it to the cabin attendant but in the excitement of being on her way to London had forgotten it entirely. Now she set it on the edge of her plate as she dropped the roll of mints back into her purse. Dan noticed, leaned forward and asked what it was. When she told him, he opened the napkin, and told her what it *actually* was.

"And you think someone on the plane working for MI-5 planted it?" she asked breathlessly.

"Yes, meaning you've been tracked ever since you arrived in London. MI-5? That's pretty sophisticated hardware you're holding in that napkin. Could be MI-5, but it could be any intelligence agency or even a private corporation that wants to track you." Dan glanced out the pub window into a small garden used for outdoor dining, recalling how he'd tracked her at the airport. Still...

Grabbing what was left of their bread, he said, "Follow me!"

They worked their way through the pub out into the garden where several redwood tables and benches sat beneath a huge oak tree. One of the tables had scraps of bread scattered across the scarred top, that a couple of crows were pecking at for their lunch. Dan walked to the table, and the birds flew away making a fuss. Quickly he crumbled the bread into small pieces, pressing the tiny Bio-tag into one of the crumbs. "It's a good thing you didn't ingest it. We'll sit at the other table and watch to be sure the crows eat all the crumbs, then we're out of here." They did and the two promptly left.

"Do you think whoever planted the device will figure out what happened to their tracking device?" Kate asked with a sly smile.

"No one ever knows for sure what their target or another agency is doing. However, I'll bet that whoever is, they will have an interesting time tracking that crow."

They drove back onto the Motorway. Kate was sleepy but too tense to sleep. The idea of having almost been internally bugged was off-putting to say the least.

"What do you know about robotics, Kate?" Dan continued.

After some thought, Kate decided not to reveal the full extent of her knowledge, intending to serve as the active agent she'd been trained to be and 'play the game' to draw Dan out further. "Not a lot, though I wish I did. My *forte* is computer science, quantum theory and nanotechnology. All close, but not specifically robotics. The only robot in my life was the one manufactured by Tolomeo Technics, and that tin bastard almost killed me. I do know enough to ask the right questions, however, if that's what you're wondering."

Dan didn't answer immediately, navigating across the Britannia Bridge onto the Isle of Anglesey then continuing toward Holyhead. Once solidly back on path, he stated that by this time the agency or company tracking the device would likely have been figured out it had been highjacked.

"They have other ways to track me, I guess," Kate offered flippantly.

"Yeah, like the guy in the dark blue panda four cars behind us."

Kat checked her side mirror. "What's a 'panda'?"

"It's a British term for a police car. That one is a Fiat Punto. Easily goes over a hundred sixty kilometers per hour— one hundred miles per hour by your Yankee reckoning. See that? They're switching it for a different car and color. They know we know they're there, but want to let us know they don't care."

"A constant escort," Kate said.

"Right up to the moment your plane heads back to the States I would guess."

Ignoring their new tail, Kate asked, "Why do you think scientists are so set on producing a race of robots that look exactly like the rest of us anyway?"

Dan shrugged. "Perhaps in the future, robots will be in control of the world. If it comes down to having robots do all the work, it would be wise to make them resemble us so we wouldn't know who the real controllers were, don't you think?"

"That makes no sense. Are you saying robots should run the world?"

"Next time around, Kate, there'll be no Adam or Eve." Dan turned into the parking lot of a small hotel facing the Irish Sea and announced, "Our hotel, courtesy of DIA."

Not far away, Dr. Gwen Evans opened the BioVault door at Jones-Llewellyn Bionics and said softly, "It's me, Terrwyn. I'm afraid I have some bad news."

Since the disappearance of Emlyn, Taff had made Gwen personally responsibility for Terrwyn. In the past, no one except himself or Emlyn had had access to Terrwyn's quarters. Gwen had worked with Emlyn on Terrwyn's overall design. As soon as Terrwyn received her next-generation 'brain,' MoD was scheduled take Terrwyn over from her.

Gwen, however, had since made up her mind that would never happen.

Taff watched on CCTV and noted, not for the first time how much alike in build and facial contours both women appeared. As he turned up the volume knob on the console, he heard Gwen say softly, "You won't be seeing Emlyn anymore, Terrwyn. He's…well, he's gone away," even though she was aware she was talking to Terrwyn in her unactivated mode. Gwen looked as if she were talking to a biological person rather than the seemingly unresponsive robot.

The scene made Taff recall the words of Cynthia Breazeal, a computer science professor at the Massachusetts Institute of Technology, who held that before long humans wold be interacting socially with robots, robots would able to read our emotions and express their own. Some Japanese researchers claimed there was a "fuzzy boundary" outside of which robots and their responses could seem *too* lifelike for some people. They dubbed it the 'The Uncanny Valley Syndrome,' noting a growing sense of unease felt by some humans who worked closely with robots over long periods of time. This wasn't true of Gwen.

"Gwen, you and I shold drive out to Emlyn's house tonight to check through Emlyn's lab to be sure there's nothing of Terrwyn missing."

Gwen jumped at the sound of the disembodied voice and went cold. "The…the house has been closed by the police," she replied unsteadily. She must stop him from finding Chadron, Terrwyn's twin. The existence of Chadron had been her and Emlyn's secret. No one else must *ever* know of Chadron, Emlyn had charged her.

"I called the police, and have authorization to enter." Taff's voice sounded hard-edged, lacking the usual soft lilt of his Welsh dialect.

Gwen had no choice. With Emlyn gone, Taff was now her sole boss. Then she remembered something Emlyn told her on one of the weekends she had spent at his home and felt stronger, knowing that though he might be head of Jones-Llewellyn Bionics, Taff didn't know everything that went on there.

"Fine. I'll get my things and meet you in the parking lot in five minutes." Dr. Gwen Evens hurried from the vault, made a quick call to Dan Blake and exited the building.

"You took your time," Taff muttered as he opened the passenger door of his black Jaguar sedan, "Get in. We don't have all night."

A. G. Hayes

Chapter 15

Kate's room had an expansive view of the sea; Dan's, the parking lot. He was in the bathroom showering when his phone rang. It was Gwen. Wrapping a towel about him, he listened for a moment then said,. "Okay, I'm on my way." Toweling off quickly, he dressed, grabbed his jacket and left for Kate's room.

"Who is it?" Kate asked, hearing a knock at her door.

"It's me. Open the door. Quick!"

Kate unlatched the bolt. The door clicked open and she peeped around the edge. "I was about to take a shower."

"Doctor Gwen Evans called from JLB. I have to go and I don't know when I'll get back. The panda that was following us is in the parking lot, so I presume the driver is somewhere in the hotel, watching and waiting. I need you to go down to dinner, get a table and tell the waiter there will be two. Wait fifteen minutes, then order and look pissed. Finish your meal, go back to your room and stay there. I'll call soon as I can." Kate started to speak, but Dan held up a hand. "Gotta go. Stay in the hotel." he reiterated, pulling the door shut.

It was almost dark when Dan hurried across the parking lot to the empty panda and slit each tire with a long-bladed switchblade.

He made it to Emlyn's house in record time after Gwen's call, the Mini quickly eating up miles of twisting back roads through the Welsh countryside. He had trained in Wales while with the SAS, and now, his knowledge of shortcuts were paying a premium. Approaching the final quarter mile of gravel up to the house, he skidded the car to a stop behind the large all-glass conservatory at the rear of the home. Cutting the engine, he eyed the looming structure with it's myriad of milkly-white, translucent glass panes. A single security light glowed from inside. Gwen had told him about a hidden key to Emlyn's private lab beneath a sizeable yellow flowerpot inside the conservatory.

Inside, all seemed quiet. Satisfied there was no one in the conservatory, Dan pried opened the door with his blade. A breath of warm, pungent air instantly swirled around him. The scent from the greenhouse plants was almost intoxicating. He quickly located the flowerpot, removed the key and returned outside.

While all the rest of the house windows were dark, he couldn't be certain whether, after Emlyn's disappearance, someone—either a policeman or an agent from one of the various intelligence agencies—might be hiding in wait. He moved quickly down the side of the house, feeling his way until he located a window ajar and was inside in seconds. Using the penlight he always kept with him, he weaved his way to the lab following the directions Gwen had given him on the phone.

The robot he was looking for, Terrwyn's "sister," was reclining limply in a comfortable chair in one corner of the lab. Dan was stunned to see how beautiful she looked. An Asian woman dressed in an ankle length green silk dress, her head was resting on a cushion, eyes closed, ebony hair tumbled about her face. She was like no robot he had ever seen or expected to see. He reached out and touched her cheek. It was warm. She moved slightly.

He must hurry. Gwen had said to hide her beneath one of the beds in an upstairs guest room, the third room on the left from the top of the stairs. Taking a deep breath, he reached down, slipped one arm beneath her legs and the other beneath her arms and back, picked her up and held her to him. Her head shifted, resting against his cheek. Again, she stirred, and her arm tightened a little across his shoulder. She sighed lightly, and as she did, he smelled the crisp, clean youthfulness of adolescent breath. This was no robot. She was as real as…

"It has been some time since I felt the arms of a man about me," she said huskily. He jumped at the sudden sound of her voice and stared into her face. Her large, green almond eyes were open and she gave him a faint smile.

"Who are you?" Dan demanded setting her on her feet, shaken by her sudden awakening.

"My name is Chadron." She reached out and ran her fingertips lightly down from under his chin to his groin. Dan felt himself grow hard at her touch. "I see you like that," she whispered. "Good." She moved closer, pressing hard against him. Dan knew at once that beneath the long silk dress there was nothing but warm tempting body. He paused. Gwyneth and Taft would be getting closer every moment. There was no way he could hide this woman under a bed and expect her to remain out of sight. He had to do something. Fast. Dan grabbed Chadron by the wrist and dragged her from the room, through the house.

"I love a strong man," Chadron exclaimed.

Dan worked the two of them through the window he'd left unlatched, exited and returned to the conservatory, pulling her inside with him. Chadron's nostrils flared at the fragrance of the plants in the thick warm air, and Dan felt a wave of revulsion course through her as she inhaled. The skin of her wrist in his hand changed from human warmth to burning fire and a flicker of dispassionate evilness flashed across her face. Instantly the Vatican briefings on alien transfers, computer glitches and INSANE robotic intelligence, plus his Jesuit training in theology and the natural sciences, came to mind. *Pure alien thought, completely indifferent to others when awakened,* he recalled being cautioned.

Chadron, sensing the change in Dan, backed away, her green eyes suddenly narrowing, pupils dilating as she hissed, "A strong *and* wise man, the latter of which I fear you are not. You realize I could have provided you the most gratifying intercourse you would ever know?" She stopped beside a long table containing flats of Fish Hook Barrel Cacti, short fat cylindrical plants, twelve to fifteen inches high, covered in spines.

Whatever was happening to the robot—and something clearly was—he needed to keep her hidden and quiet until Taff and Gwyneth checked out the lab and headed back to Holyhead. He moved slowly and as unthreateningly as he could toward Chadron, fully intending to bind and gag her, then slip her into his car. If what he had just seen was alien thought or even possession of an artificially intelligent being—and he strongly thought it might be the second—it was and would be a prize for the Vatican far beyond a king's ransom. Chadron waited until he was almost up to her, then turned, scooped up one of the cacti, the bristles penetrating her hands seeming not to bother her, and hurled it into Dan's face.

Reaction honed by years of training allowed Dan to raise his arms in a protective cross just before the plant struck, the fishhook-like spines piercing his hands and wrists, stinging like hot needles as she ran past him and out the door.

Dan attempted to grab her with his spine impaled hands, but was too late. She'd vanished. Seconds later, he heard a car crunching up the gravel driveway. Dan shut the door and hid out of sight. He'd failed, and now, because of him, there was a self-contained humanoid robot on the run. Alternatively and much worse, an alien AI. As soon as Taff and Gwen passed, he made two quick phone calls, the second to Kate waiting back at the hotel.

Approaching from the front door, Taff and Gwen navigated the house to Emlyn's lab, where Taff began checking over various items and schematics scattered on a workbench. Intent on confirming there was no connection between them and anything in progress in Holyhead, he almost didn't hear Gwen ask, "Is there anything I can do to help?"

Taff removed the top of a cardboard shoebox sitting on the workbench; he didn't answer as he lifted a pair of women's shoes from the box.

"A pair of woman's shoes," Gwen said nonchalantly, her stomach secretly knotting.

Taff grunted and turned them over, checking the soles and size.

"They've never been worn," he concluded, a look of puzzlement on his face.

"Perhaps they were meant as a present for someone. May I see them?"

Taff passed them to her. Gwen examined them and nodded. "Prada. Very expensive. Yes, I would definitely say a gift." In fact, they were her exact size. Her's, Terrwyn's and Chandon's.

Taff grunted. "Emlyn didn't have any women friends as far as I know," he said, his puzzlement turning to suspicion.

"Maybe they were for someone he'd known in the past, and he'd simply forgotten about them," she replied, handing them back to Taff.

"If so, why keep them in his lab? I'll take them back to the office. There's nothing else of interest here." Taff checked his watch, adding that, as they were on the premises, he wanted to take a quick walk-around.

Gwen's heart skipped a beat, wondering if Dan had been able to hide Chadron upstairs. "This is a big house, Taff; why don't I check upstairs while you go through the ground floor rooms. We've been here almost an hour and it's time we got back."

Taff hesitated, then agreed. "Okay. Meet me at the front door when you're through."

The first room she checked was the third on the left—the guest room where she had told Dan to hide Chadron. She checked under the bed. No Chadron. "Shit." Had he placed her in the wrong room or run out of time and put her in any available room? She checked the other bedrooms. Nothing, again. Was it possible Dan hadn't yet arrived? No, he *must* have come before them because Chadron was not in the lab when she and Taff entered. That was, however, all she knew for sure at this moment. She walked to the top of the staircase and listened. She could hear Taff downstairs banging around. Whatever had happened, it was time to get Taff out of the house. Gwen made a last quick check of the upstairs rooms, this time looking inside the wardrobes. Still nothing. Then she heard Taff call from the front door. "Gwen! Let's go. It's starting to rain and will take us even longer to get back."

"Okay," she called back, wondering what in hell had happened to Dan and Chadron.

Chapter 16

Sunset glinted on the dome of St Peter's Basilica as Fr. Enrico Conti entered his office in the Pontifical Academy of Science building in the Vatican gardens. As he sat, his phone rang and he scooped it up.

"Echo," a voice said on the other end. The call sign immediately grabbed his attention. It meant he was talking with Dan Blake.

"It's started, Father." Dan quickly brought Conti up to date on his encounter with Chadron and her disappearance.

"Contact Dr. Gwen Evans and tell her the Manchester meeting is off," replied Conti. "I do not want either of you near the place with that robot loose."

A click and a dial tone on Dan's end indicated the call was over.

It was late in London, and the antique shop was swathed in darkness except for a dim light from a single desk lamp. Daphne Delferholm stood motionless beside the rocking horse, then, slowly pushed it into motion. Its rocking shadow magnified onto the wall, swaying back and forth in a gentle hypnotic rhythm. The phone jangled, causing a startled Daphne to jump. She answered it on the third ring.

"Yes, Father? Of course. Come over right away." She let the phone clatter onto the base. Fr. Amorth had sounded agitated. Daphne had no idea he was even in the country.

Five minutes later a taxi pulled up, and Daphne quickly unlocked the front door, holding it open for the priest to enter.

"Upstairs, quickly! And turn off that light!" the priest ordered. Daphne hurried as best she could, though being in her early nineties, she and stairs were not a good match. She grunted her way up to the living quarters as he pulled out a chair in the upstairs kitchen. As she sat, he brought her up to date. "Daniel contacted the Vatican. He says he has seen, with his own eyes, a robot that was likely under control not of its human creators but of itself or an alien life form. Whether that control is being exerted from outside or inherently from within due to an INSANE process, it is the embodiment of what we most seek and at the same time most fear. It would be proof of what we've suspected for so long, and present the ultimate challenge in terms of saving its soul, if it indeed has one as we suspect."

Daphne sighed. "Well, we both knew it was only a matter of time." In fear, her mind slipped sideways, and she began reliving the days before and during the war as he continued to speak.

"This is the second actual eyewitness report by one of our own," he finished excitedly.

"Where did they occur?" Daphne asked, returning rather reluctantly to the present.

"Wales."

"First at Jones-Llewellyn Bionics," Daphne guessed, wanting confirmation.

"Yes. The second time at Doctor Eric Sykes private lab. The government sealed it off the moment he disappeared." The priest sighed and leaned back in his chair, his face drawn and tired. "There was no need for us to send an agent to the lab; we already had someone inside: Doctor Gwyneth Evans, one our scientists worked on the JLB staff and also knew Sykes. At more than a collegial level, I might add."

"Why weren't we informed, Father?"

"It was, at the time, considered wise not to. That is all I can say at the moment."

"Wait, Father. If I recall correctly, you said the robot escaped from Daniel while he was in the conservatory at the Emlyn Llewellyn' home." Daphne leaned forward. "That means…" she began, completing the thought a moment later, "…no one knows there is a second robot of any kind outside of the JLB Lab in Holyhead. Not even Taff Jones."

"'A riddle. wrapped in a mystery, inside an enigma'," the worn man admitted, quoting Winston Churchill.

On her way back to the lab with Taff, Gwen was doing her best to remain calm, while Taff rattled on about the red shoes. "Emlyn was always a stickler about security, and then we find these shoes. Could he have had a woman staying with him? Perhaps he was unknowingly entertaining an industrial spy?"

"That pair of women's shoes on which you're so fixated could mean anything or, just as likely, nothing at all. Was Emlyn in the habit of entertaining women at his home? Everyone knows the answer is no," Gwen stated, feeling a headache coming on. "If in fact he did, it would be just as much a surprise as learning that he had a fetish and liked to wear women's shoes in private. Come to think of it, having Sykes actually spend a weekend at his place is a surprise, don't you think? Emlyn was a *very* private man." She hoped as she misled him that Taff would never find out about the times she and Emlyn had spent together at the house. Gwen closed her eyes and tried to relax, focusing on the repetitive sound of the windshield wipers, while her mind drifted back over the months since she had joined the team at Jones-Llewellyn Bionics. Being a spy was terribly stressful. All she wanted right now was to get home and go to bed.

The phone jarred Kate awake. It was Dan. He said he

needed to speak to her after having just speaken to Fr. Conti. Still half asleep, she learned of his unusual encounter with Chadron. "Get dressed, Kate, and meet me at the back of the hotel. Bring all your stuff. I'll be there in five minutes. Oh, and stay in the shadows."

Kate hung up and moved fast. She was at the back of the hotel a minute before Dan's Mini crept into the parking lot with its lights off. On their way to what he said was a safe house, he brought her up to date.

"The disappearance of Dr. Llewellyn and the presence of a highly intelligent, perhaps fully conscious, self or even alien-controlled robot on the loose that can't be distinguished from a human changes everything, including your schedule, Kate. Your cover as a reporter is now on hold until further notice. We are going to follow Dr. Llewellyn. As we speak, he's being moved 'just in case' to different location for a couple of days."

Kate pulled her collar higher around her neck. "So you've known Doctor Emlyn Llewellyn's whereabouts all along? And Tolomeo?"

Without answering, Dan continued. "As I said before, don't get any ideas about going after Tolomeo. I need you to put your scientist hat back on."

"Meaning what, exactly?"

"You have a doctorate in computer science, right?"

"You know I do."

"Well, you're about to get the chance to apply your expertise and study the workings of Chadron, as soon as we talk with Dr. Llewellyn and determine her likely whereabouts."

"Chadron?"

"Terrwyn's runaway 'sister' robot. As soon as we can locate her."

"I see I need to remind you again: Computer science is not the same as robotics, Dan."

"Still, I'm sure that it will prove a great help."

Kate sighed, "How?"

"Jones-Llewellyn Bionics incorporated some very advanced computer designs in their latest models."

"Most robots today do."

"Yes, but we're talking 'Star Trek' technology, Kate."

Kate noticed his demur manner had changed and all semblance of humor was gone. "Go ahead, Dan. Tell me."

"We've been ordered, as I said, to check in at a safe-house. When we leave after the meeting, I'll be authorized to bring you completely up to date at last."

Chapter 17

At two am, Gwen received a phone call at home from the Vatican instructing her to call the night operator at the JLB lab and say she would not be in due to a home emergency. A car would pick her up in five minutes.

Chosen for their ordinariness, safe houses like the one located at Number 17 Ackroyd Terrace in Llandudno, forty miles from Holyhead, was among MI-5's finest. A three-story stone Victorian, with a grey slate roof punctured by multiple chimneys, the whole surrounded by a small front garden, it's lace curtains in no way belied the cellar's soundproof firing range, and Gwen was about to receive a course in the use of small arms from her ostensible MoD intelligence service employer.

"Anything here look familiar?" the instructor asked, indicating a row of handguns.

"They're all pretty exotic looking. I guess that one over looks the least intimidating," she said as she pointed. "It looks closest to the Webley my dad had in the army."

"Close enough," the instructor chortled, noting the complete lack of similarity. "This one's a semi-automatic, nine millimeter Smith and Wesson M&P 'Shield'." Under normal circumstances, a thorough course in weaponry is a required part of any agent's training. In Gwen's case, as a scientist, her Vatican assignment had been to provide feedback on progress at the two labs. Except for two people at 68 Via Condotti, no one so far was aware Gwen was a double agent working for the Vatican's Servizio Informazioni del Vaticano or SIV and that she could easily have given tips to the arms instructor standing before her. Now that she was going into the field with Dan and Kate, the UK authorities decided Gwen should at least know one end of a gun from the other.

"I'll now provide you with some basic weapons training; then you will fire a few rounds from the weapon you selected and that will have to do."

Gwen nodded innocently, and the instructor went quickly through care and handling of both automatic and single action handguns. Fifteen minutes later he said, "Let's try a few rounds, then, shall we?"

Gwen hefted the 9 mm Smith and Weston M&P 9 Shield in her hand and stared down range at the paper targets."If you really think I'm ready, I'll take a go at it."

"You'll do fine. Remember the stance I showed you and

relax." He was referring to the classic two-handed Weaver Stance where the dominant hand is used to grip the weapon with the other wrapping around the dominant hand. The instructor placed a sound-suppression headset over Gwen's ears. "Always use these on a range; otherwise you'll go prematurely deaf."

Gwen rolled her eyes, chambered a round, took aim and squeezed off a shot.

"Not bad, though I'm afraid you'd be dead, Luv, if the target was shooting back at you."

Gwen grimaced and reloaded. "Dan Blake, he's good at this, is he?"

"I've never seen anyone better with an automatic. Now try again. Bend the knees a little more this time."

Gwen copied his stance, holding the revolver steady in both hands.

"Try several shots, taking a half breathe between them."

"Much better," the instructor said, after she'd discharged the entire nine rounds.

"Not if she were aiming for a kill." Dan interjected, having approached quietly from behind. He smiled slightly, hands on his hips. "I'm going to have to work with this lady a bit. Mind if I give a hand?"

"Not at all, sir. She's a fast learner, this one," the instructor said, moving away.

"How fast am I supposed to learn, and what's the latest from Father Conti?" Gwen hissed.

"*Very* fast. Father Conti says sooner the better."

"That's why I was told to call the lab, say there was an emergency at home and then was brought here?"

"Yes. Are you sure you were believed at the lab?"

"No."

Dan picked up a 9 mm Beretta from the table and handed it to her, "Come on; let's make some holes in the targets." Side by side, they sighted on the paper targets with the outline of a man's head and shoulders. "Do what they taught you in Rome and surprise the hell out of the instructor, " he whispered, stating louder, "Okay, do it now."

Gwen did. Six bullet holes appeared in the heart area of the target. They walked back to the astonished instructor and Dan handed him the Beretta. "You must be one hell-of-an-instructor. She's *really* improving fast." Dan and Gwen left through a heavily padded soundproofed door, and walked upstairs to the living quarters, where they entered together into a tastefully furnished living room.

Kate and two men were already present. Kate was sitting in a leather armchair. A tall, thin man stood in back of her, staring out of the bay window. He turned and faced Gwen when Dan and Gwen approached. "Ah, Doctor, please sit down." He indicated a high-backed couch fronted by a glass-topped coffee table. Gwen and Dan sat side by side; the tall man remained standing. "Soon you will meet with Doctor Llewellyn. He's safe, well rested, and as you've undoubtedly figured out, in no danger."

Gwen leaned forward eagerly. "Where is he? I'd like to speak with him now."

"Um, not right away, I'm afraid," the tall man answered. "He is still undergoing intensive debriefing; I will, however, inform him you are relieved to know he is safe." He glanced at Kate, then at Dan. "You two: There is to be no mention of his safe return. It must remain a secret known only to those of us in this room." Assured, he turned to Gwen. "Doctor, you'll come with me. Blake, you and the young woman will follow. We will go in convoy."

Dan secured his seatbelt as they tumbled along in his Mini along a rutted country road behind the lead car. "Okay, Kate. We're both aware that bioengineering over the last twenty years has successfully duplicated how neurons in the brain behave when we move any part of our body; this has led to demonstrations of technology that may eventually restore full movement to the immobile. The new frontier is in duplicating how neurons in the brain behave when we think. Especially when we're conscious."

Kate looked at him askance and said, "What brought that on?"

"I promised you the rest of the explanation I began earlier in the car. The British government wants this particular aspect of robotic research and development kept secret. Of course, DIA also wants a piece of it along with who knows how many other nations. For *sure* the Vatican wants it." He paused, "Kate, what I ran into at Emlyn's place is a cut far above *any* human today."

"For a layman you're certainly well up on neuroscience and bioengineering."

"Thanks. To be completely honest, the Vatican spooks proved expert in fast, well-grounded training in anticipation of what I would likely encounter. But they knew I would need the support of someone with a richer scientific background." He glanced in his side mirror.

"So, you are a double agent," Kate concluded.

"We live in a global village these days, Kate. Double agent, triple agent, quadruple agent—what's the difference as long as the agent is equitable as far as information goes. Besides Kate, like you, today's intelligence agencies more and more prefer to work with people with an occupation that does not reflect secrecy."

"When do I meet my co-scientist?"

"You already have," Dan muttered. "MI-6 knows this car, so we play the fox while they play the hounds, and the car in front proceeds to its destination."

"And that will in no way deter MI-5's ability to tail us or the car in front of us," Kate snorted.

"Oh, I don't know. For one thing, the car ahead does not contain Dr. Gwyneth Evans."

"Where is she?"

"En route to the Vatican."

"I'm impressed. So Dr. Emlyn Llewellyn must be waiting at the Vatican, right?"

"No, he'll remain in the UK for now."

"You mean you've known all along where he is!"

"Not exactly. We'll be meeting him in a day or so." The car ahead turned right, and Dan continued straight ahead. "Back in the fifties, the American dream turned a gun on itself and now, sixty years later, we see the result in an entirely different generation of politicians."

A. G. Hayes

Chapter 18

Alone in his office, Grainger Milburn squinted through an aromatic blue haze at the decoded message in his hand, taking particular note of the last sentence; *Number 68 insists on absolute secrecy until further notification.* He leaned back and closed his eyes.

As a young captain in the US army of occupation in Europe, Grainger had met Madam Louise Zander when she was merely Louise Zander, an eighteen-year-old French woman, working for British Intelligence during the war as an underground resistance member. Grainger found her smart, intelligent, and fully able to kill a man quickly, silently, and without qualms. His association with Louise became the reason he had decided to later become an intelligence officer with DIA.

They quickly became lovers, and for two years remained deeply involved in research regarding Hitler's Final Solution, a term used widely at the time to indicate atrocities committed in Nazi death camps toward the eradication of Jews, gypsies, Slavs and other groups deemed to be humanly inferior to Hitler's Aryan super race. Medical experiments, including various methods of sterilization and gene splicing, were carried out in the name of eugenics, the "science" of optimal self-directed human evolution, an effort that grew in popularity from the late nineteenth century to the mid-forties, then slowed after the war, when it became synonymous with Nazi atrocities.

Hampered by world reaction, eugenics faded from the public heart and mind. However, eugenic research continued covertly, and in the early part of the twenty-first century, Number 68 via Condotti had clamped the lid on its own investigative findings. Milburn studied the full text of the coded message.

> *There is increasing indication that a similar form of life is breeding with humankind to create a human free from disease, with a mind far superior than any of us can imagine. As far as the human race is concerned, few are aware of this, and many of those in charge do not wish their constituents to discover this, leaving the politicians with sufficient plausible deniability to deal with the situation. We are in the process of of being recreated by other beings, not just for our*

good but also for theirs. The Vatican is aware that Papal authority will have no place in this new world, and organized religion as we know it will soon vanish.

Milburn slipped the message into a burn box and tapped a button twice in quick succession, turning the document to toast. His thoughts flashed back to Edwards Air Force Base where he had been present when President Dwight Eisenhower arrived with his Secret Service security team after being called away from a dinner in Palm Springs on February 20, 1954. When the complete entourage had assembled in the hanger, they were individually sworn to secrecy as to what happened next.

The event proved to be the most significant that any American President could have conducted—an alleged 'First Contact'—a meeting with extraterrestrials that portended the beginning of a series of meetings with different extraterrestrial races leading eventually to a treaty of sorts.

The First Contact Meeting had occurred with extraterrestrials who possessed a distinctive though alien "Nordic" appearance. However, any agreement with what reminded humans at that time of a race of Aryans, was uniformly spurned. This First Contact, was, however, exactly that, and a series of meetings followed that led to a treaty signed with a different extraterrestrial race dubbed the Greys.

The stated—and one must surmise unstated—motivations of the different extraterrestrial races involved in the treaty discussions still caused Grainger to awaken nights in a cold sweat.

Grainger knew that if the truth of what happened during those times got out, it would panic not only the US population but that of the entire world.

Nonetheless, over the years, partial word slowly began leaking out from conspiracy theorists and UFO believers, in most instances eventually being ridiculed and called fantasy, imagination, fake news and other kinds of idiotic blather. The government quickly embraced the new game of social name-calling as far as it helped keep the truth under wraps. Now, over sixty years later, the event was still considered a popular myth and little else.

Milburn relit his pipe, well aware that a new and unique development in human history had taken place. Labeled initially a "global political awakening," it was brutally suppressed by all governments as a common threat to national power. The term, coined by Zbigniew Brzezinski, former National Security Advisor of the Carter administration, referred to the fact that, for the first time in history, almost all of humanity was simultaneously becoming politically conscious and politically active. Global activism was re-interpreted and quickly repurposed as a pathway toward universal cultural respect and economic opportunity in a world still deeply scarred by memories of World War Two. In doing so, it became a grave challenge to globalization by the economically elite. In response, the economically elite were said to be seeking a way to reconstruct the world into a global New World Order

Grainger's perspective by way of his age, knowledge and experience made all this more apparent to him, and a thin smile crossed his lined face. Brzezinski was a political genius, but it was only, Grainger recalled, when authorities in a singular confluence of needs, wants and desires, decided that robotic eugenetics could be used to hearld the New World Order that the "shit truly hit the fan." If robots could be made so human-like as to be biologically indistinguishable, the world would have a number of walking laboratories from which to choose the best results.

Simultaneously, the extraterrestrials and Earth's bioengineers had begun providing the elites alien, human and human-like robots as a way to direct and control society in ways never before imagined, the most distressing endgame being the global socio-scientific dictatorship many feared since the early decades of the twentieth century. The planet had now become embroiled in a complex political maelstrom of unprecedented ferocity.

Grainger sucked his an empty pipe, imagining the

breakup of the basic human family unit. The pact the US government had made on behalf of the world over sixty years ago at Roswell with the Greys portended the transfer of individual selection to non-humans for selective breeding in exchange for rapid humanoid evolution and advanced technical knowledge. Suddenly it all seemed less dazzling. What kind of world were he and his colleagues about to usher in?

Chapter 19

The tension in Taff's office became onerous.

Sykes growled, "I don't know about you, but having two key personnel out of the lab at once bothers me."

"Gwen called in that her mother is ill."

"And Emlyn? He's been gone almost a week and still no one has a clue what happened to him or where he might be. Has it occurred to anyone here that a competitor could be mounting a takeover?"

Taff bristled. "Yes, it has, Sykes. Very much so. But until we receive definitive word—we wait. The authorities are doing all they can."

Sykes glowered. "What about Emlyn's housekeeper? What's her name?"

"Collins. Morgana Collins," Taff snapped. "What about her?"

"She might know more than she told the police, you know, about that phone call the morning he went missing."

Taff shook his head. side-to-side. "The police checked and rechecked her story; she definitely received a call from the house the day Emlyn vanished."

"But no one knows for certain *who* called," finished Sykes. "That woman knows more than what she's said so far."

Taff shrugged. "Possibly." Sykes was getting on his nerves and Taff was beginning to rue the day he'd become involved with Sykes and Tolomeo. Emlyn's disappearance had pushed his already fraught nervous system close to a breakdown. Months after months of of 12 and 14-hour days working on Terrwyn's design and the constant pressure from Whitehall were taking their toll. He needed time to think.

The next words spoken by Sykes proved a Godsend: "Listen, Taff. I know you are tired and worried about Emlyn and Gwen, but I just got an urgent call from my company to get back to Yorkshire. They're sending my 'copter. A couple of problems at the lab need clearing up. You know how it is. A few days, then I can be back here. By then, we should know more and we can hopefully sort things out. "

"I hope so," Taff muttered, more relieved than he wanted to let on. "While you're gone, I'll get in touch with Gwen to see how her mother is getting along."

Sykes glanced at his watch. "Well then, I'm off. Let's stay in touch at least once a day." As soon as Sykes left his office, Taff grabbed his phone and dialed Gwen's home number. It rang six times before an older woman's voice answered.

"Yes, this is Gwen's mother. Whose calling, please?" said a delightfully cheery voice on the other end.

Taken by surprise, Taff answered, "Doctor Jones. May I speak to your daughter please, Mrs. Evans."

"She's not here, doctor. Is everything all right?"

Hearing the genuine concern in her voice, he replied, "Gwen said you were ill and she needed time off to take care of you."

"I may be old, but I'm not ill. She and I spoke on the phone last Sunday as we always do."

Taff's shoulders sagged. First Emlyn, now Gwen.

"Has she gone missing or something? What's going on?" Mrs. Evans voice wailed.

"Listen to me, Mrs. Evans. There has to be a reason why she called in and left work. Are you alone at home?"

"Yes. Oh, my! What could have possibly happened?"

"Stay at home and don't worry. I'll take care of everything. I'm going to send someone over there right now, understand?"

"Yes, doctor."

"Good. Now, don't worry. As I said, everything will be fine."

Taff hung up and called the police, officially reporting Gwen as missing, and, rethinking things, requested a police doctor attend to Mrs. Evans and stay with her until further notice. He knew the police were in constant contact with government security, and both could move fast, particularly when not one but two scientists working on a top-secret project abruptly go missing.

Chapter 20

Former US President James Madison, in his *Political Observations 20 April 1795* stated that of all the enemies to public liberty, war was the one most to be dreaded for it inevitably resulted in the many being dominated by the few. To this, the modern Church would add that only when humans take full responsibility for their evolution, could there be a basis for defeating war. To this, Morgana Collins, in her own, far simpler way, would add that unless individual people took action towards establishing that day, the word *human* would become history.

Morgana Collins could have made a simple phone call and the search for the two missing scientists would have been over. However, she had made a call already—from Emlyn's home to hers on the morning of his disappearance. She did it to do her individual part towards insuring that humans would never become cyborgs. She did it so if the police checked, they would discover the call record. She did it so she could honestly say that her phone had rung at her house, she had received a brief set of instructions then had hung up. For her small, but pivotal, individual part in the abduction of Emlyn, Morgana remained silent and well paid.

Chapter 21

A rainless but extremely humid summer had lowered the flow of the River Tiber, leaving behind a rotting admixture of grass and mud. The imposing silence was suddenly broken by the roar of a helicopter descending from high above. On touchdown, a slim figure dressed in a lime green flight suit jumped nimbly to the pad. Head low, her long blonde hair swirling about her, Dr. Gwyneth Evans scuttled across the helipad escorted by Vatican security. Within minutes, she was inside The Pontifical Academy of Sciences in the Vatican gardens.

Father Enrico Conti was in his office reading a report when he heard the sound of the helicopter approaching. He turned a page and continued reading. Advanced Industrial Science and Technology Corporation, located outside Tokyo, had just announced plans to sell a line of 158-centimeter "fashion-bots" for around $US 200,000 each. "Thousands of humanoids could be working alongside humans in less than a decade, if that is what society wants," stated Fumio Miyazaki, corporate Chief Engineer and Professor of Cybernetics at the Toyonaka Campus of Osaka University. "If the world is ready for a functioning robot secretary, for example, there is no need for a major technical breakthrough."

Father Conti glanced at his watch, then read further. A Tokyo subsidiary of Hello Kitty, Sanrio Kokoro, had just announced production of advanced, conversational, life-size humanoids. "Robots have hearts," Kokoro Planning Department Manager Yuko Yokota was quoted as saying. "They do not look human unless we install souls in them. When manufacturing a robot, there comes a moment when the light flickers in its eyes, and that is when we know our work is complete."

Public opinion in Japan may be open to robots mumbled Conti to himself, *but in the rest of the world, science fiction movies such as* Blade Runner *and* Terminator *continued to conjure images of armed robots forcibly taking over the world.*

"Thanks to such benign cartoon characters as Astro Boy, Japanese people have a friendly image towards robots," said Toshiba's Yoshimi Asada, according to the article. "Japan's indigenous animistic belief system might also have readied people to accept human-like robots with minds of their own. Everything has a mind—the mind of the lamp, the mind of the chair, the soul of the desk," he said. "Therefore the machines should have their mind, too. If we proceed in this study, who knows, machines may have something close to a human mind."

At the sound of approaching footsteps, Father Conti removed his reading glasses, closed the report and leaned back, folding his hands in his lap and waiting for the knock at his door.

"*Entrare*," he called. The door opened and two men in well-tailored suits entered. One took a position slightly in front of the other and stated in Italian,"We have have with us a British guest."

Conti raised a hand. "Then we must all speak in English."

The closer man nodded and signaled for Gwen to enter.

Pushing back his chair, Fr. Conti rose. "Doctor Evans. Please do sit down. It is nice to see you again."

Gwen slid into a chair facing his desk as Fr. Conti continued, "You look as though you could use a cup of real Italian coffee."

Gwen's eyes brightened. "An expresso would be much appreciated."

"I understand you were not fully briefed before you left for here."

"I was told you would bring me up to date."

Conti nodded. "You are here for two reasons: One, our communications have been compromised. Second, I would like you to escort someone back to the UK."

A tap on the door interrupted him. "*Entrare.*"

A thin, brittle-looking, middle-aged nun dressed in a grey habit entered, carrying a demi cup of steaming pungent coffee which she placed on the desk. Bowing slightly, she said, "She is ready, Father."

"Thank you, Sister." Conti indicated to Gwen to take the mug and follow the two men and nun. Gwen had been in the building twice before, the last time was before going to China to work in the Tsun labs. Together, the trio entered a well equipped, modern cybernetics laboratory, and were led to an adjoining room designed for core staff meetings. Gwen stopped abruptly on seeing the solitary occupant seated at the table. It was Chadron.

Gwen glanced at Conti who was the last to enter, then she went directly to Chadron who remained unmoving, staring straight ahead. After the nun in grey left the room, Fr. Conti spoke softly. "You may approach her, doctor. She has been well taken care of and is in perfect working condition, I assure you."

Gwen reached out, gripped Chadron's right arm just above the elbow, and squeezed lightly three times. Chadron's eyes opened and her head tilted to the side as she looked up at Gwen, a glow of recognition lighting her eyes. Her brows tightened and a restrained smile crossed her lips.

"Where am I, Gwen?"

"With friends. I have come to take you home."

"I remember having to escape. I ran, but they found me. I had to…"

"It's alright," Conti interrupted. "You did what you were trained to do, Chadron. Doctor Emlyn is very pleased." Conti edged away and muttered to Gwen, "I was told she looked and fought like a devil processed with super human strength when they found her."

"It is her nature. She is programmed to maximally resist if taken against her will."

The priest sputtered. "Her 'nature'? Her 'will'? Terwillyn and now Chadron were supposed to be only minimally functional demonstration prototypes…"

"Yes, Father, I know. I helped design her." Gwen checked Chadron over closely, her fingertips running gently across the humanoid robot's shoulders and arms. "Who shut her down?"

"I don't know. When she arrived, she was as you saw her on entering the laboratory."

The inquiry itself seemed innocuous, but no one except herself and Emlyn supposedly knew Chadron even existed, so who *had* shut her down was a cogent question. Had it been Emlyn? Gwen triple-pressed a point on Chadron's other arm, and Chadron once again became motionless.

Gwen stood back and drained her coffee. "Okay, then, how did she get here, Father?"

"She came to us from the UK by a private jet that landed

at a small airstrip outside Rome. She was transported from there to here by helicopter."

"A Vatican helicopter, I presume?" Another cogent question.

Fr. Conti nodded affirmatively. "It was decided she should be brought here for…testing. When finished, we decided you should return together on a commercial flight to the UK. Our tests indicate she is constructed such that she should be able to pass through airport security and passport control without setting off any alarms, but our security people demanded *in situ*, realtime confirmation. If, as we suspect, robots like Chadron can defeat airport security and passport control…well…surely you understand what this means…"

Gwen finished the last of the thick black expresso, and placed the tiny cup and saucer on a side table. A breeze fluttered through an open window behind her carrying with it the odor of the river outside. After a few moments of silence, Gwen asked, "Why was she *really* brought to Rome, Father? She has been missing for over a week."

"Surely you know better than to ask a question like that, Doctor Evans." Working for the Vatican SIV, one did not ask. One carried out orders without explanation.

Conti rubbed his hands together and stared at his plump palms. "You and," he nodded at Chadron, "will travel together by Air Alitalia to London Heathrow." His brown eyes hardened. "If you pass through passport control and security without a problem, you will have greatly helped our understanding of these unique...individuals...and ultimately our cause."

"And if we don't? What then?"

"Much thought has been given to this test. Both of you will be dressed as Muslims, your faces covered by *burqas*. You will each be accompanied by an SIV security officer. If any problem arises, rest assured the remainder of your journey back to Jones-Llewellyn Bionics will be without further delay."

Gwen knew the skin—technically the epidermis— covering Chadron's body was not only life-like to the touch, but had been specially manufactured to nullify all known passive electronic sensors that might otherwise trigger a security alarm. In addition, a standard airport x-ray scan, when attempting to probe beneath her skin, would return a data package that, on the receiving screen would instantly decrypt to look to the sensors like an average female human body. MoD had insisted on this feature which utilized a three-dimensional holographic program implemented by Emlyn. But Gwen had had a different agenda in mind when she wrote it. It was her job to preserve and protect Chadron, and that meant making certain that Chadron never arrived back at Jones-Llewellyn Bionics. They would somehow both have to vanish after arriving in the UK.

Chapter 22

Immediately prior to leaving the safe house, Dan received fresh orders from Grainger Milbourn. Kate and Dan were now dressed in foul weather gear, sailing NNE in Dan's boat up the UK coast, sipping hot tea.

"Out of the many scenarios I imagined on this assignment, none of them included sailing in a small boat in rough seas off the coast of northern England," Kate groaned.

Dan gripped the galley table with one hand and poured her more tea. "You never know in this business." The staccato sound of Morse code dots and dashes began beeping from the speaker of their shortwave radio located alongside the GPS and VHF communications equipment on a shelf over the chart table. Dan slid into the seat facing the radio, grabbed the Morse key, and clicked a reply while Kate watched in fascination. She knew about Morse code from her grandfather but had never experienced it in use. Dan and the sender responded back and forth for a couple of minutes, and then with a flourish, Dan sent a close signal and leaned back in his chair.

"I thought that had gone out with black and white TV. How can anyone learn all those dits and dahs? They sound the same to me. Besides, why would anyone use Morse code in the first place?"

"More people than you think still use it because first, it's direct; second, it can cover long distances without loss in signal clarity, and finally, we know of no Morse code hackers as of yet."

"Can't anyone just tune in and listen?"

"Not when we're communicating narrow beam in cipher Morse," Dan explained with a sly smile.

"So what was that all was about?"

"We're going to meet a man about a robot."

"Where and when?"

"Fleetwood, Lancashire." Dan nodded toward the chronometer. "We should be there in about five hours."

"Good. It'll be daylight by then."

Dan grunted. "And we'll need every ounce of morning light we can get. Too many ferry boats running back and forth between Ireland and Fleetwood to take a chance at night; we have to be able to see the marking buoys when we make our approach. I'm going to put my head down for a couple of hours."

"You're going to sleep while the boat is sailing with no

one in charge?" Kate asked with trepidation.

"The sails are trimmed and we're on auto steering. The wind vane will slavishly adjust for any wind shifts. I have all top of the line equipment. It'll do a better job than most humans, and do it hour after hour without tiring or making a mistake." Dan climbed into his bunk and was asleep in seconds.

For Kate, the rocking and pitching of the boat, the sound of the bow rising and slapping into the waves was unnerving. The idea that the "captain" had gone to sleep had taken her close to panic for a moment. Then, lying on the top of her bunk, she stared at the roof of the cabin in the dim light cast by the tiny light bulb over the chart table and told herself if Dan could sleep, she should.

Kate was still awake when Dan stirred. "Get some sleep?"

"No. I stayed awake and kept this tub upright by sheer will power."

He laughed, then stood, stretched, slid back the hatch and checked the sky. "It'll be dawn when we make our approach to the Fleetwood Lighthouse. You can still catch a few hours of sleep before we begin docking." Looking back at Kate, he was surprised to see her fast asleep. Dan turned up the collar on his Henri Lloyd Voyager jacket and squinted into the mist slowly melting from solid black to translucent grey.

A. G. Hayes

Chapter 23

Jilly Suede jumped, spilling champagne over the rim of her glass and onto her dress when the phone rang. "Hello," she answered after putting down her champagne glass and patting her dress with a napkin. "Who is this?"

"Are you all right, Ms. Fannon?"

"Damn it, Hank! Where are you?"

"I'll be back tomorrow." Jilly hung up without another word. They were both wise to phone taps.

Many of the abandoned textile mills of nineteenth-century Yorkshire had been renovated into smart condominiums, others into business office buildings. Eric Sykes owned such a structure in the center of what was now the extensive Nano-Comp UK campus. It was a rugged stone building standing five stories tall beside the River Aire and, because of the advanced computing going on there, was known locally as HAL after the computer aboard the spaceship in the hit movie *2001*. In fact, most of the staff were graduates of

Leeds University School of Advanced Computing, several with with second PhD's in biologically constrained neural network modeling. Divided into teams, they worked on the top floor, the most highly secure floor in the building. No one entered without passing through multiple high-tech security checks. Sykes touched down on the heliport atop the imposing structure a little after six in the evening. Bending low, he dashed from his company's Augusta A109 helicopter, his hair streaming in the downdraft from the slowing rotors and headed for the rooftop entrance to his office. A steel door swung open as he approached and a cheery voice said, "Welcome back, Sir."

Sykes handed his attaché case to a young, dark-haired woman. "Did Marcello call?" he asked, referring to Father Vincent Marcello SJ, a Society of Jesus Professor of Theology and Modern Politics within the Inner Realm, a mixed group of theologians, cosmologists and scientists working together in service to the Vatican. Fr. Marcello was said to have experienced a close encounter of the third kind while a young student Jesuit in Padua in 1967, and for the next 45 years, had spent his life in the study of what the Church formally called "the occult," including historical Satanism and after-life beliefs, while amassing information on the invasion of the human race by powers known and unknown. His special interest was, in his own words, "soul jacking."

The Vatican had created the Inner Realm led by dedicated Jesuit ethnologists to investigate reported UFO sightings and abductions, in the process addressing the secret fears of many who sought to reflect the statements of the increasing number of simple-minded hysterics and heretics. Only the Pope himself, Father Gabriel Amorth S.J. and three trusted Cardinals knew the Inner Realm even existed.

"Yes, he asked you to call him as soon as you arrived."

Sykes eased into his black leather chair and reached across the desk for the secure phone.

"He said to recite this to him this over the phone." She passed him a slip of paper.

"What's this? It looks like a password."

"He said you'd say that, and to just do it, Eric." Everyone at Nano-Comp UK called him Mr. Sykes except Donna Harcourt, his secretary of the last four years, who called him Eric. He called her Miss Harcourt—except in bed.

In his office, he dialed the number and read in a slow monotone the combination of letters and numbers on the slip of paper, then said, "Sykes here. I just got in." After listening intently, he replied, "Yes I understand perfectly. Goodbye," and hung up saying, "Things are moving faster than I thought, Miss Harcourt."

A. G. Hayes

Chapter 24

Rain slashed at him in a solid sheet encouraged by a sudden, harsh westerly wind as Dan tied the sailboat in a slip in Fleetwood harbor. Kate looked on miserably.

"Okay. It's time to check in with the Harbormaster. Come on, Kate."

Kate followed him, head down into the driving wind and rain, to a nearby green door that in the current deluge looked more like a waterfall. The door opened, parting the waterfall and slammed behind them as a gust of wind pushed them inside. A woman at a computer looked up. "Can I help you?"

"I want to see the Harbormaster," Dan said, the two shaking the water from their slickers onto the floor, much to the receptionist's dismay. .

The woman peered over the top of her granny glasses. "I'm sorry, but he's not here."

"When is he due back?"

Removing her glasses, the woman sighed. "Never, I'm

afraid. He's dead."

"What happend?"

"Are you a relative or...?"

An inner door in the office behind her slid silently open, and a thin-faced man in a dark suit peered in. "It's alright, Mary. Let them in."

"Come in, come in," the man invited, waving at Dan and Kate to join him in a small conference room that overlooked the harbor. It had once been the Harbormaster's office, and was replete with seascape oils on the walls, nautical furnishings and the smell of pipe tobacco.

"Take a seat." The man indicated two heavily-used, brown leather chairs in front of the desk. Lowering himself into his own battered swivel chair, he gave a tired smile. "I work with Whitehall, which is all that you really need to know at the moment. The man you were supposed to meet did, in fact, die in this room a few hours ago." Kate glanced around the room searching the floor nervously.

"There are no blood stains or yellow police tapes, Ms. Keenan, and no TV reporters outside with news vans to waiting to report anything."

Dan shifted in his chair. "I need to see some identification. I can't just take your word that you're 'with Whitehall'."

The man nodded. "Of course. Grainger Milbourn told me

you would ask for such." He pushed a phone across the desk. "It's a dedicated line. Pick up the receiver. I won't be offended."

Dan picked up the phone handle and, after a couple seconds, engaged in conversation, after which he glanced at Kate, nodded affirmatively and returned the handset to its base.

"Your contact died a natural death. He had a history of heart trouble, and suffered a heart attack in this chair where I am now sitting," the thin man said, tapping a bony finger on the desktop directly in front of him "Mary found him and called us."

Dan leaned forward, "And where exactly do you fit in?"

"It matters not, except to tell you I am for the moment your combined government *and* Vatican contact for now."

Kate glanced askance at Dan.

The sound of a vehicle and squeak of brakes caused Dan to turn and look out of the window. A dark green van appeared from out of the rain and came to a stop.

"Ah, that will be your ride."

"What about our luggage?" Kate asked.

"Your luggage is already being transferred into the vehicle as we speak. We must hurry. Time is of the essence. Please follow me." Standing, the thin man turned and left the office through a private back door, Dan and Kate following.

"This downpour continues all the way over the Pennines and into Yorkshire," the thin man shouted as the three loaded quickly into the van. The shorter and stouter driver and the taller thinner man accompanying them were both in their mid-thirties; the driver told them they would be in Yorkshire in a couple of hours where they would be brought fully up to date. Kate stared out of the rain-streaked windows. She had always wanted to visit the Yorkshire Dales and Herriot country. She had been an avid fan of the TV series *All Things Bright and Beautiful*. At this moment, however, nothing about them looked bright or beautiful.

The rain finally slackened as they entered the small market town of Skipton in Yorkshire. The thin man informed them they would be staying at The Craven Heifer, a small hotel in the town center. He carefully omitted mentioning that the reservations were courtesy not of MI-5, but of Britain's foreign Secret Intelligence Service, MI-6, which had only recently taken notice of what had the appearance of a foreign intelligence operation.

Check-in was fast and efficient. The two men escorted them to their rooms, informing them their luggage would follow. Dan and Kate's rooms were both on the first floor, but four doors apart.

Kate glanced at Dan before entering her room. "I'll give you a call on the house phone after I freshen up," she said, shutting the door. Switching on the light, she surveyed the comfortable furnishings including an inviting, four-poster bed.

Slumping on the its edge, she closed her eyes and relaxed, soaking in the silence. The last few days had been hectic, almost non-stop confusion. Her reverie was interrupted by the sound of a harsh voice. A powerfully built man in a black rain slicker had silently entered her room.

"Good evening, Kate. There's been a change in plans."

She remained silent, never moving her eyes from the intruder.

"Don't you want to know who I am?" he asked.

"The last few days have prepared me for almost anything," Kate said, measuring the distance between the man and the brass lamp stand at the bedside.

"Good. I'm here to take you to your next stop." He waved a hand when she began to speak. "There's a car waiting downstairs."

Kate looked him in the eye. "I'm not going anywhere. I've had enough of this cloak and dagger rot. My job was to interview business leaders in the world of computers and robotics, not take part in some horse-shit, wild goose chase!"

"I'm sorry to hear that," the hulk said, crossing the space separating them in a flash, plunging a hypodermic needle into the muscle of her arm while placing his other hand over her mouth. Kate tried to scream but couldn't. She struggled, but it only made the drug work faster and she crumpled onto the bed. The man replaced the hypodermic syringe in it's leather pouch and the pouch into an inner breast pocket. Calmly collecting Kate's purse and umbrella, he flipped open his cell phone. "She's on the way, Doctor Sykes."

Chapter 25

After his abduction, everything for Emlyn was a blur. He had awakened in a small room, lying on a lumpy mattress. Easing from the bed, he groggily crossed the room and peered through a smudged windowpane of an upper room. In the distance was the sea. But where exactly was he? And what had happened? His head was thick and his mouth felt like dry cotton and sandpaper. Turning back into the room, he eyed the bed, a wooden chair and a small table. He staggered to the door and turned the knob. It was locked. He pounded on the door and yelled for help in a voice cracked and hoarse. There was no answer. Where was he? The last thing he remembered was going to the kitchen to get a cup of coffee. Emlyn returned to the bed and slumped on the edge, took a deep breath and fell back helplessly across the mattress.

A few hours later he re-awoke to the sound of the door opening. A thin slice of light slanted into the dark room. Someone was standing in the doorway. A soft click and light abruptly filled the room.

Emlyn shaded his eyes and saw a small man with a snow white mustache leaning on a wooden walking stick. "You are in no danger, Doctor. You are under government protection."

"Protection? Protection from what?" Emlyn spluttered.

"You will be brought up to date soon. Come with me," the man said, inviting Emlyn to follow him out of the room.

Moments later, Emlyn was staring into a brandy glass, swirling the dark gold-brown liquid. He switched his attention from the glass to the woman opposite him.

"Madame Louise Zander," she said softly by way of introduction.

"I wish we had met sooner. Here we are sipping fine brandy while the entire British security service searches for me, and, thanks to you, they haven't a clue where I am. For that matter, neither do I."

"Simply put doctor, they actually have more than a clue to your whereabouts. You are under their protection until such time as MI-6 decides to collect you." Madame Zander watched his reaction as she spoke. An expert in such games, she felt a surge of satisfaction trickle through her thin frame. Reaching to a side table, she opened a silver cigarette case, removed a Galouse, and placed it into an ivory holder between her lips. Emlyn noted the silver cigarette lighter on the table, quickly reached it and snapped it on, holding the flame beneath the tip of her cigarette. With a thin, claw-like hand, she grasped his wrist and touched the cigarette tip to the flame. Her next words issued from within a cloud of blue smoke curling around where her head had been. "When you were taken from your home, it was MI-6 who arranged it." She knew the information would shake the man and that was exactly what she wanted.

Emlyn took a long sip of brandy and rolled his lips together before saying calmly, "And why would they do that?" while his mind flashed back and forth wondering about the safety and secrecy of Chadron.

Madame Zander appeared from within the cloud of smoke and blew a perfect ring, silently watching it evolve. "To be certain that no one would find out about that second piece of wonderment you developed in secret in your home laboratory. The government takes extraordinary measures to be aware of all, shall we say, 'extracurricular activities' of its scientists."

Emlyn grimaced from the acrid smell of the French cigarette. Coughing, he waved his hand in front of his face. Louise continued, aware he was attempting to change the subject. "Rest assured doctor; your secret is safe with us."

"You have it?"

"Yes, if by that you mean the cyborg we found unharmed and tangled in a thicket near your home. We have secreted it to a secure location."

"Where is she?" Emlyn demanded, feeling his world

falling apart. He was doing his best not to show any emotion, but as far as Madame Louise Zander was concerned, he was doing a poor job.

"You will see it…her…soon enough."

Chapter 26

Father Thomas Conroy PhD SJ closed his eyes and relaxed in the black leather seat of the fast-moving car as it sped through the British night. Father Tom, as his close colleagues called him, was slimly built and sported a signature grey crew cut. When he walked it was with an energetic spring. In short, he was a man whom some in the Vatican thought decidedly out of place in a religious environment. These days, however, there were increasing numbers of others like him, researching areas that for hundreds of years had been off limits to holy men older and far more reverent than Father Tom Conroy with his doctorate in astrophysics. This new breed of priest had first begun to appear at the Vatican in the late eighties. The older, more conservative—some would say reactionary—priests openly considered Conroy and his ilk on a par with the Devil. But with time, there were fewer and fewer of the old guard. The aging old men sat in the shade in the Vatican gardens during the summer, thumbing through their breviaries, muttering Latin and sipping tea. Winter found them indoors, seated in groups like thin crows hunched over some road carrion, and treated like old folks in a retirement home.

Fr. Conroy had spent the last twelve years working on the Vatican Advanced Technology Telescope on Mount Graham, home of the international astronomical complex operated by the University of Arizona at Tucson. The director of the Vatican Observatory Research Group was retiring later in the year, and Conroy would take over. He could then have authority over and direct access to the Vatican Advanced Technology Telescope (VATT) and the world-renowned Large Binocular Telescope with Camera and Integral Field Unit for Extragalactic Research (abbreviated oddly by the church L.B.T.W.C.I.F.U.E.R. and concatenated, to the older priests' consternation, to LUCIFER) located adjacent to the on-campus Steward Observatory. LUCIFER, a twin-horned mirror system was being used to monitor a secret, deep-space, advanced Vatican program. It included an Alpha Magnetic Spectrometer similar to the one located just outside the International Space Station, and was in constant communication with the ground-based CERN project team in Europe. Fr. Tom was not just another parish priest visiting Rome.

The voice of the driver caused him to open his eyes with a start. To his surprise, he'd fallen asleep. "You have a call, Father. The telephone receiver is located inside your right-armrest."

Conroy scooped up the phone. "Conroy."

He recognized the voice at once when it answered, "Enjoying your trip to the UK, Father?"

"Daphne Delferholm, how are you? It's been years."

"Yes, it has. I thought you were in Arizona."

"Daphne, you know better than to lie to a priest," he said with a smile. "We're hard to fool, having heard them all in the confessional."

He heard a soft chuckle in his ear before her reply: "I'm told we will be at the same meeting tomorrow, and thought I'd let you know Madame Zander will be with me."

Conroy paused, his mind attempting to sort out why Zander, of all people, would be present. "Sounds interesting," he replied, peering out the window only to see his reflection as the car sped on through the darkness. The Vatican had called tomorrow's meeting in a hurry. He would have been back in Arizona at this moment if Rome had contacted him an hour later.

Daphne's voice was in his ear again. "Do you know what tomorrow's meeting is about?"

"Not yet, Daphne, but it must be of particular import, seeing we are meeting in the Jodrell Bank Office at Manchester University. Not knowing is the safest way to keep everything secret."

"I was also told we were going to visit with someone from Google Alphabet's Deep Mind, Kings Cross, Father."

Conroy tensed. There had been no previous discussion about a visit from the Deep Mind people. "How did you get this phone number, Daphne?" he asked in retrospect.

"As you said, Father, not knowing is the best was to keep a secret."

A dial tone replaced her voice.

Returning the receiver to its armrest, he once again closed his eyes and sat back. Jodrell Bank Observatory, located in Cheshire, was headquarters for a £1.3 billion project to build the world's largest radio telescope. The new headquarters at the Jodrell Bank Office had quietly opened in January 2012, superseding the existing project office at the University of Manchester.

An agreement to run the Square Kilometer Array (SKA) from Jodrell Bank had been signed by Australia, China, the Netherlands, New Zealand, South Africa, France, Germany, Italy, the UK and, of course, the Vatican, which had provided much of the seed money. It was rumored that the most likely site for the actual array would be either Australia or Southern Africa though the location was as yet unannounced and presumably undecided. SKA was designed to answer several key questions about the universe, beginning with the origins of life, both human and alien.

There had arisen doubts over its future in recent years, however. Identifying the spacial origins of the aliens currently on earth manipulating the human genome—information deliberately withheld from humanity—had begun taking second place to the effects that increasingly conscious humanoid robots could potentially have on human society. Conroy and other scientists had discussed at length the fact that robots were becoming self-aware, agreeing that, in time, they would begin questioning their role in human society and purpose within the universe. With self-awareness, it was further assumed they would learn to access the internet—that sum total of everything known to and imagined by humans, and they could begin to reprogram themselves, perhaps even begin creating other robots "in their own image." The looming question was, of course, what these "servants" would ultimately think of their human and alien masters. Wouldn't the faults of the masters become glaringly apparent? Wouldn't the servants want or even feel obligated to "fix" their faulty masters? Would self-consciousness bring with it a soul? It was the Church's ultimate responsibility to protect and nourish the soul, preparing it for the afterlife. Was there be an afterlife for robots and aliens? There was nothing in the Church's liturgy that specified that only human's could have souls and those souls reside in an afterlife.

As a consequence of these discussions, Fr. Conroy had

developed an alternative theory, wondering when the first robot became *fully* conscious if spirituality and religion would be any part of its awareness? Religion, as he saw it, was more of a human "social club," whereas spirituality, increasingly ignored by the Church, was its fundamental currency. The Vatican's discussions surrounding this issue of which he was a pivotal part, were creating the most challenging assignment he had ever drawn: developing a way to insert into a robotic "mind" a program to teach it about God and the importance of its soul, be that soul ultimately human, robotic, extraterrestrial or some mixture thereof. Doctor Eric Sykes efforts at Nano Comp UK were foremost in his mind as he mused what a robot with true self-awareness, a knowledge of religion, a sense of spirituality and a soul would be like.

Returning for a moment to the extraterrestrial "problem," the ability to study the origins of extraterrestrials and their civilizations using the world's most powerful radio telescope could be a million times more informative than anything thus far provided. If only the Church had begun the project earlier and they had already gathered sufficient information on extraterrestrials before their presence had become known. Fr. Conroy sighed, and reclosed his eyes. The visit with Deep Mind would be most interesting.

Chapter 27

The first thing Kate's bouncing, drugged body could focus on was a hazy image of a distant house. As her vision cleared she noted Yorkshire stone walls, a slate roof and two chimneys spewing ragged, windblown smoke across a grey morning sky. It was the type of house one would expect in a gothic novel. Kate shook her head and refocused on the building. Was she dreaming or was this real? The moment she realized it *was* real, she knew she was in trouble.

"Not far now," the driver said. "We'll soon be inside, and can have a nice cup of tea." The driver swung the car into a narrow driveway bordered by high bramble bushes and drove toward the house standing alone on a small rise surrounded by moorland countryside stretching horizon to horizon. Kate's flexed her fingers and hands, to her surprise gripping her umbrella. When the car came to a halt, she glanced up in time to see a lace curtain swing back into place in a window on the second floor.

The car door opened and the smiling face of Eric Sykes peered at her. "Forgive the intrusion into your schedule, Miss— I'm sorry, I meant to say Doctor—Keenan, but there seemed no other way I could talk with you."

He was charming, and for a second her guard dropped, though she remain silent.

"You are in no danger I assure you."

Kate, however, was in no mood for empty reassurances. "Then why was I drugged and hijacked?"

"We have an acquaintance in common, Doctor Keenan: Hank Tolomeo; I was informed you knew each other but would be apprehensive about meeting him. You do remember him, don't you?"

"Tolomeo is here?" Kate asked, a cold shudder seizing her.

"He will be soon. He's quite looking forward to seeing you again face-to-face."

Kate pressed back into the car seat. How did Tolomeo know about her being in the UK?

It had been over a quarter hour since they had arrived at the Craven Heffer, and Dan was hungry. He rang Kate's room, but received no answer. Frowning, he headed down the hall, knocked on the door, called her name and was about to put his shoulder to the door when the floor service attendant appeared in the hallway. Dan turned toward him. "Did you see a young woman go downstairs?"

The man nodded at the room door. "She left with a gentleman a few minutes ago…in a car."

"Did you happen to notice the license number?"

"No. We do not make it a policy to intrude on our guests," the man said with a touch of indignation. Seeing Dan's obvious displeasure, he added, "I did see a four-door sedan driving away from here immediately afterward."

As soon as the man left, Dan took out his cell and made a call.

Grainger Milburn was about to leave for the day when his phone rang, and eyed it suspiciously before picking up. "Milburn." As he listened, he reached into his jacket pocket for his pipe. His face tightened as Dan brought him up to date from his and Kate's experience at the harbormaster's office to Kate's disappearance.

"This is the first I or anyone here in MI-5 have heard about any harbormaster dying. Who arranged the trip to Skipton?"

Dan's heart sank. *"You don't know?"*

There was no immediate answer. What Dan heard were the sounds of Milburn going through his pipe cleaning, packing and lighting ritual. "Dan, there are people in this business who know a lot; some, more than others. Then there are the 'Mandarins'. They decide what will eventually be known to the rest of us."

"Like leaving you out of the loop about the dead harbormaster," Dan grated.

"Dan, I am being put out to pasture. It's a miracle I know as much as I do and that I've lasted as long as I have on this operation. Josh Rivet is taking over. I'll make some calls and get back to you."

Dan began to speak, but Milbourn cut in. "Keep your head down and wait for my call." The phone clicked and Dan, irritated, slipped the phone into his pocket. No way was he going to sit and wait. He had a bad feeling and decided he needed to locate Kate. Now.

Josh Rivet shrugged off his jacket, tossed it over the back of a couch and was on his way to the drinks trolley when his cell chirped. "Rivet." He listened while pouring two fingers of Johnny Walker Black. It was MI-5 agent Jack Drummond. "Milbourn brought me up to date on Blake's call and the disappearance of the Keenan woman."

"You know where Tolomeo is?" asked Rivet.

"Yes. He may be on the run, but he has his fingers in a bevy of international shell corporations, many resulting in control or outright ownership of many of the world's best robotics companies. It also turns out he's a long-time associate of Doctor Eric Sykes," Drummond replied.

"Right. Sykes runs Nano-Comp U.K. outside of Skipton.

Let me guess: Sykes is in Yorkshire. He's slippery, that one," Rivet stated. "It's going to take more than research and surveillance to know what Tolomeo's up to. Move in on Sykes right away."

"We'll have him in the next few hours," Drummond replied.

Rivet finished his drink and poured a refill.

Sykes watched his man search and disarm Kate, smiling at the result. After a moment, he ordered, "Give me the umbrella." Kate's heart pounded as the man took it from her and handed it to Sykes, who scrutinized it, running his hands carefully along the furled waterproof cloth.

"I purchased it a few days ago in London."

"Very nice, indeed," Sykes replied. "Handy this time of the year." He aimed the umbrella as if it were a rifle; then, in one movement unsnapped the restraint snap and pushed it open. Kate's heart skipped a beat as he spun the umbrella, then rested its shaft on his shoulder. "You made a good choice."

Kate held her breath as he held the shaft loosely in his left hand, released the canopy button and folded it back into furled position, snapping it closed. "Definitely well made."

Kate breathed an inaudible sigh when Sykes laid it aside having never triggered the cunningly designed switch.

Sykes turned to the man standing to the side. "Find out why it's taking so long for Tolomeo to get here. You'd think the man was traveling here from India…"

Kate suddenly recalled Tolomeo's connection to her former India lover and tormentor, Kumar Pashagora, and froze.

Tolomeo sat hunched in the back seat of his car parked at the side the moorland road on a bleak expanse of the West Yorkshire moors. Rain, thunder, and flashes of lightning added to the misery of his crouched driver, who was struggling to change the right rear wheel. Pulling his coat collar up around his chin, he cursed, hoping he'd be meeting Sykes in a warm dry place and soon.

The two government agents followed Tolomeo with the lights off, remaining back a quarter of a mile, the storm aiding their cover. The driver, despite being trained in such tactics, had, because of the weather, found it a difficult task. Pulling the car to the side of the road he muttered, "They've stopped." The second man snapped, "Then we wait." Both were under orders from Jack Drummond.

The driver leaned forward squinting through the windshield. "They've got problems."

A shaft of light flashed from the distant car's interior as the passenger car door opened.

"Someone's walking past the tail lights and removing something from the trunk. A tire iron, I think. Maybe they have a flat." They'd stopped their car a few feet short of the top of a downward twist in the two-lane road.

"Leave our interior light off, and when I get out, release the handbrake. I'll give the car a push, then jump back in. We can coast silently down the hill. Shouldn't take much; we're on the crest."

After pushing the car into motion, the speaker scrambled into the back seat.

"Now what?" the driver asked as the car silently rolled down the hill.

"Drive close as possible to the left side of their car, I'll have the side window down and when we are parallel to their car, I'll 'dart' the driver. Then you stop the car and do the same to the passenger."

In the UK, traffic drives on the left side of the road and the driver sits on the left side, so the situation was perfect for such a maneuver. The man in the back seat checked the pneumatic pistol that would shoot a ballistic device loaded with an immobilizing drug. The "bullet-syringe," propelled from the gun by means of compressed gas would be quick, silent and effective. The vehicle gained speed as it continued to roll down hill.

Tolomeo's driver had finished tightening the last wheel lug when a rush of air slammed into him. He reached for his neck, tensing momentarily from the pain and succumbed to blackness. Tolomeo had no time to react before his door was ripped open and someone entered in a blur. The dart entered his neck, half an inch above his collar bone. Within seconds, both unconscious men were half a mile up the road in the MI-5 agents' car.

Chapter 28

Dan presented his identification card at the hotel desk, and minutes later had obtained Sykes' local address. The hotel manager, a young man, could not do enough for Dan after he had seen the government identification card—even offering to drive. "In this weather, Mr. Blake, the house you're looking for would be difficult to find. It's in an isolated location on the moors." Dan knew he was right and agreed. The young man, eager, star struck and desperately wanting to be part of a governmental intrigue got his heart's wish that day.

In darkest night, on a narrow strip of road in a fierce lightning storm, speeding over hills and through tight bends, the young man rattled non-stop about what an exciting life he thought Dan must be living, how he had seen every 007 movie several times, how much he would like to join the government's security service and asked what he had to do to apply.

"How much further?" Dan interrupted.

"Less than fifteen minutes, Sir."

As they literally flew over the top of a hill, Dan noticed in the distance a car pulled over to the left side of the road, interior lights on, front and back door open.

"Pull over there."

That same moment, Sykes glanced at the clock on the mantle. Tolomeo should have been at the house twenty minutes ago, and the man he'd sent to locate him had not reported back.

Perched on the cushion edge of a winged chair next to a glowing coal fire in a mantled fireplace, Kate feigned self-righteous indignation. The thought of Tolomeo or Pashagora reentering her life caused her mind to race out of control. Unable to force herself to pause and think, pure self-preservation provided the necessary trigger for survival.

Kate ventured, "Perhaps Tolomeo has changed his mind, or decided to wait for a better opportunity or safer location. It could be he knows something you don't."

Sykes glowered. "He'll be here, and you'll leave with him." His cell phone buzzed. Snapping it open, he moved to the far side of the room. Kate could not hear his voice, but from the man's increasing frown had a hunch it had to do with Tolomeo's continued absence. Eyeing her purse and umbrella across the room, she made up her mind that she would never again allow Tolomeo to hurt her. She was tired of the all the damned silly spy business and being tied continuously to Dan as if she were a schoolchild. There had been too much drama as far as she was concerned, from the meeting in the antique shop to present, and she was smart enough to know that everyone she'd met so far was using her for one or another purpose. But for what? How did it all fit together? What was the ultimate endgame? She knew more than she did when she started, but answers to these two most important questions still escaped her.

Dan checked the empty car, noted the lug wrench beside the replaced tire, and decided someone had come along and given the driver and possibly a passenger a lift. He jotted down the license plate number as a flashlight beam bounced along the car and came to a stop in directly in his face.

"Find any clues did you, Sir?"

Dan turned his face away, trying to erase the residual red blot obstructing his vision. "Turn that off, damn it! I can't see a thing with you shining that flashlight in my eyes!"

"Sorry, Sir. Just trying to help, Sir," the wanna-be agent, apparently mollified, replied.

"And get me to Sykes house fast as you can."

On the other side of the Pennines, Father Conroy glanced at the phone in his hotel room as it rang and picked it up. "Conroy."

The voice at the other end was hurried. "You'll be contacted regarding the meeting. Stay where you are until further advised." Not allowing an answer, the phone clicked to a dial tone.

Fr. Conroy pulled aside a heavy brocade curtain and stared out across the rain-drenched city of Manchester. In the background, he could hear the BBC evening news reporting an outburst of riots in the streets of Jakarta on the passenger telly. He let the curtain swing closed, reached for the TV and snapped it off, recalling his last meeting at the Vatican, and the words of the Monsignor in the wood paneled lecture hall: "Pope Benedict XVI's resignation and his enigmatic life as Papa Emeritus has inspired myriad conspiracy theories. It is time to put them all to rest." He stopped to let the recalled words sink in. "A cloned slave race is about to replace us because we have become too rebellious a people." The Monsignor had paused just long enough to assess his audience's incredulity, then continued. "Just as management is beginning to replace the working class with robots in order to extinguish labor's demands for more rights and a fair share in the profits, executives have begun clearing the path for the eventual replacement of both workers and management with bio-engineered humanoids." Murmurs from the audience. "While distinctly humaniod, they will, nonetheless, be little more than automated mind-controlled robots." Stunned silence followed. What Conroy and others had heard was a briefing on programmed humans versus human-made robots, or worse, robots designed and created by robots or aliens.

Conroy sighed. Recalling the lecture tired him and made him wish he were back in Arizona.

A. G. Hayes

Chapter 29

"The house is just over the next hill, Sir. We're almost there." Bretton Miles, "assistant agent," said courageously directing the car into near-opaque fog in an effort to try to make up for the flashlight error. He was doing his best to sound confident.

"Turn off the lights, Bret," Dan ordered. "Drive slowly. Get close to the house and stop. When I get out, drive back to the hotel and say nothing to anyone about where I am. Got that?"

Miles began a flustered reply, so Dan reached across him and snapped off the headlights. "Slow down and don't run us off the road."

Bret Miles, turning the car turned around, vanished into the foggy darkness, leaving Dan crouched just inside a high privet hedge. He remained motionless, rain dripping from the brim of his cap. He had no doubt Sykes' house and grounds would have a state-of-the-art security system.

Taking two deep breaths, he eased foreword. A shaft of light appeared from an upstairs window. A backlit shadow crossed the windowpane then disappeared. This happened several more times, leaving him to wonder if there were more people in the house. Another light, this time from a downstairs window snapped on, and Dan froze in place. When the light went off, Dan relaxed his grip the 9-millimeter in his pocket with its safety off. A damp, chill wind raced across the moorland and swirled around the house. Glancing down before easing foreword, Dan noticed an otherwise invisible trip wire made fortuitously visible by the row of dew drops coursing its length. He dropped to a defensive crouch and, following the wire, approached a military-grade fence topped with barbed wire topped with infra-red cameras.

Kate looked up as someone entered the room. Sykes was still on the phone. The place was brimming with moving shadows; the flickers from the coal fire in the grate offered no help in distinguishing who it was. Then a voice in the room caused her to shrink back in her chair. It had an accent she hoped to never hear again—that of the young Indian, would-be underworld magnate and former lover, Melhi Pashagora.

"It has been a long time, Kate, and this time you *will* return with me to India, one way or the other," he said in perfect King's English.

The accent she once so enjoyed sent a shudder of loathing

through her.

"I don't know if you realize, but once again, you have been set up, Kate. This time you are a pawn in a deadly international scheme to resurrect Tolomeo Technics and reassert it in the world of humanoid AI robotics. Your future now depends on the information you have in that singular brain of yours regarding what everyone attempting to use you is up to. You know, you should never have sold your original program for converting screenplay script into live action appearing movies to the American government. It was repurposed by the military into a base program for AI robots. That makes you the mother—the Eve if you will—of a new kind of sentient life that no one wants to acknowledge. Everyone for whom you think you're working wants only your knowledge and expertise."

"'Everyone' meaning you and that heinous villain, Hank Tolomeo? Don't come any closer, Melhi! Stay where you are." Kate's voice, flat and cold, caused the man to pause and remain a shadowy form just outside the fire light.

Sykes crossed the room, "Damn it, Melhi! I told you to stay in the other room!"

A strong gust of wind shook the house causing smoke to momentarily flow back down the chimney. The resulting scurry of ash spilled onto the hearth and in the flare of light, Kate saw Melhi's face, a little fuller but still attractively handsome. His cold jet-black eyes fixed on her as he approached. Melhi Pashagora, the son of Kumar Pashagora—owner of the largest film company in India, the man who had ordered his son to kill for her computer program, a program destined to put film companies throughout the world almost instantly out of business.

"Don't come any closer!" Kate warned, moving across the room and away. "I loved you, and you almost killed me!"

Sykes started to speak, but Melhi ignored him. "That was two years ago, Kate. As I said, your program became the breakthrough that AI scientists the world over needed."

Kate fumed. At university, Melhi Pashagora had been a trusted computer student who she'd fallen in love with at UCLA. It was he, however, who tried to steal the computer program she'd pioneered. For a moment, she flashed back to a deserted section of Highway 101 in southern California where Melhi threatened to kill her, and a battered old truck, containing two scruffy men had pulled to a halt, held them at gunpoint, and threatened to kill them both. In the moment, Kate had grabbed Melhi's gun, turned it on the two men and escaped, leaving Melhi and their two assailants at the side of the road.

Sykes snapped on an overhead light revealing a tableau of Melhi standing half way across the room, and Kate against the far wall, wild-eyed. "Kate, Kate, Kate. Haven't you wondered why you of all people were chosen to poke into our business under the guise of a reporter?" Sykes growled.

Kate turned her gaze to Sykes and stared at him. "I *am* a reporter."

Sykes turned to Melhi. "Enough of this. Get your bag Melhi. We're leaving."

"What about our meeting with Tolomeo?" Melhi replied.

Kate cut in. "I told you he would never show up. Too many chances of being taken down." A look of concern passed across Sykes' face, then he ignored Kate and once again commanded Melhi to get moving.

Dan edged along the side of the house until he came to the main driveway. Two cars stood in the shadows. Moving forward he touched the radiators of both and decided the Land Rover was the latest arrival. He also noticed the keys were still in the ignition of the Jaguar. He opened the driver's door of the Jaguar and took out the keys. A stab of light issued from the house as the front door swung open, causing Dan to dive behind a thick bush. Three figures came out the house: Kate, definitely a prisoner, and two men. Dan pressed deeper into the shrubbery and listened carefully to their conversation to get the gist of what was going on.

"Come on," Sykes whined,"we don't have all-night."

Kate gripped the handle of her umbrella tighter and prayed she and Sykes would drive away in Sykes Land Rover without Melhi. Dan heard a car door slam and the Land Rover's engine come to life. Its headlights pierced the darkness as the car crunched down the gravel driveway.

Dan next heard a string of muffled curses, as Melhi, in the Jaguar, rummaged through the interior trying to locate the keys. Suddenly, the driver's door swung open, and Melhi shot out heading back inside the house. Dan snaked out from behind the bushes into the driver's seat, started the engine, and, headlights off, accelerated down the driveway spraying gravel and mud in every direction.

Chapter 30

The Vatican is aware that Papal authority will have no place in the new world order with its mixture of humans, humanoid AIs and aliens. Organized religion as the world had known it for millennia is poised to vanish.

Grainger Milbourn had incinerated the Vatican message in his burn box but the words remained with him, ricocheting back and forth within his mind. Reaching for his pipe, he stopped, picked up his phone and called Louise.

"This is a pleasant surprise, Grainger. You're lucky I was still awake."

Milbourn smiled. "That is exactly why I called you at four-thirty in the afternoon."

They both chuckled.

He continued. "You do still eat dinner, don't you?"

"Ah, well, yes and no."

"Perhaps, with age, we have both become light dinner eaters. Nonetheless, how about a bottle of Chardonnay del

Salerno and Cornish Lobster Cannelloni with purple sprouted broccoli, turmeric, coriander and almonds?"

There was silence, then a lighthearted laugh. "Grainger Milbourn, you old rascal. What is the occasion?"

"Let's just say it's for old times sake."

Louise's mind crept back over the years to when the two had been passionate lovers. The last time they had sat in a restaurant as a couple, the odor of war still hung in the air. Peacetime caused a separation that had grown into decades.

"I can pick you up at seven. We will dine at my club."

At eight, Grainger was topping their glasses for the third time. "To 'old times', Louise."

He poured with a steady hand, she noted. Louise asked what he planned to do after his imminent retirement.

"Plans for the future?" He shook his head side-to-side, "Not exactly. Well, that is not entirely. In truth, I asked you to dinner partially to pick your brains."

Louise smiled.

"Partially," he reiterated with emphasis.

She smiled again. "About what, Grainger?"

He reached across the table, and they clinked glasses. "The Vatican Secret Service."

Louise sipped her drink, never taking her eyes off Grainger Millburn. "Have you suddenly begun going to church every Sunday, Grainer?"

"Afraid not," he said.

"Have you made friends with a particular priest?"

"No."

"Then I must introduce you to one," she replied. Louise finished her wine, picked up her large leather handbag from the floor beside her chair and rummaged through it. "Is this a smoking or non-smoking restaurant?" she asked.

"This is my club, Louise. We do whatever we want."

"Good." Within seconds, blue smoke enveloped the table and Grainger was flung back to the 'good old days' by the smell of her French cigarette.

"My God, Louise, do they still make those things?"

"Do you still smoke that smelly pipe you were always relighting?"

Grainger refilled their glasses. "Tell me more about this priest."

"His name is Father Conroy. He's a Jesuit."

"Ah, and this 'Soldier of Christ' knows his way around the Vatican battlefield?"

"Especially so, yes. Also, he knows contacts who, as we both know, would not be loathe to work with people with cloak and dagger skills to execute hands-on field operations when required."

Twirling the stem of his wine glass for a moment, he remained silent, lost in thought.

Louise nodded. "So you remember, Grainger?"

"I certainly do. The Sodalicium Pianism," he said softly, referring to a low-profile group in the Vatican, which had been taking care of the Vatican's 'private interests' since the middle ages. He and Louise had together clashed briefly with the S.P. just after the war while working in Europe. Grainger had barely escaped death at their hands.

"Where is this Jesuit Father?" Grainger asked.

"Manchester, last I heard. He was there to attend a meeting."

"What does he do?"

"He runs the Vatican Advanced Technology Telescope on Mount Graham, home of the international astronomical complex operated by the University of Arizona at Tucson. At least, that's what he does ostensibly. Father Tom Conroy is not just another parish priest." Louise sat a little straighter in her chair. "You have all but retired from the company, Grainger, so why the sudden interest in the Vatican?"

Grainger's gaze swept the dining room of the Special Forces Club or SFC, a private club located at 8 Herbert Crescent, Knightsbridge, in London. There was no sign outside the building indicating the club's presence nor would there ever be. The SFC was founded in 1945 by surviving members of the Special Operation Executive (SOE), sometimes called Churchill's Secret Army, other times referred to as the Ministry of Ungentlemanly Warfare, or the Baker Street Irregulars. The Club was intended by its founders to be a meeting place for both those who had served in the SOE and for members of similar related Allied organizations. This tradition continued, with an unusually close relationship with their US wartime counterpart, the Office of Strategic Services, or OSS. Club membership included holders of the Victoria Cross, George Cross, and the George Medal. Unlike many other clubs open only to male officers, the SFC welcomed all ranks and women, reflecting the membership and spirit of the SOE. Oddly enough, this was Louise's first visit.

Grainger returned his attention to Louise. "I need to know more about what the Vatican is up to the field of modern robotics and why."

"Grainger, this is the Church you're talking about, and we are both approaching our eighties. What would you expect to find?"

"Being old fogies will be to our advantage. Anyone over seventy is invisible in today's world, and as long as we don't have to chase over rooftops or drive in high-speed chases..."

"We?" Louise exclaimed, stubbing her cigarette in a glass ashtray.

"We could do our investigating as an elderly couple. Travel first class wherever we go."

Louise lit another cigarette.

"Think about it, Louise; it would be like the old days during the war."

"Once again, for whom do you imagine us working and what exactly would *we* be investigating?"

Grainger didn't answer. He didn't need to. He'd already made contact with his opposite in position and rank in the Vatican Intelligence Agency, technically the Servizio Informazioni del Vaticano or SIV and it was sufficient to assume Louise was already anticipating this. As soon as he convinced her, they would travel to Rome where they would be greeted publicly as elderly pilgrims.

"I should like to contact Father Conroy and see what he thinks of all this."

"Don't mention any of what we've just discussed, Louise. I want to get the feel of him firsthand."

Louise snorted, "I have much experience in such things, Grainger."

"Yes of course, but I must reiterate how important it is for me to assess Father Conroy myself before we share anything of what we've just discussed with him."

She reached into her leather purse, pulled out her cellular phone, dialed Fr. Conroy's private number and held it before him.

Grainger sighed. "Very well, but just to humor you."

Chapter 31

Melhi's Jaguar was a late model, meaning Dan could not drive without at least the driving lights, which he reluctantly tolerated. The Land Rover was nowhere in sight. The road was a simple *tarmacadam* slash through the wild wind-swept heather. The Jag surged through the storm, and Dan felt a sudden stomach-churning swoop when the car became momentarily air-born as it blasted across a humpbacked bridge. In the far distance, town lights raised Dan's hopes. If he could find some local help, he might be able to find out where the Land Rover had gone. As he drove closer he recognized he was on the outskirts of Skipton; the distant lights were of the town including his small hotel. Not bothering with going to the car park in the back of the building, he braked outside the front door and hurried inside.

The place was quiet as a tomb. Dan tapped a small bell. "Hello? Anyone here? Hello? Hello?" He went behind the counter into an untidy office. A telly was playing, and a man was fast asleep, his shoes propped on a messy desk.

Dan slapped the desk. "Wakey-wakey, chum!"

The man jumped, almost falling over. Recovering, he pushed back from the desk, only to fall sideways in in his haste. All he could manage was, "Who? What?"

"Get the manager. Now!" snapped Dan. "National emergency."

The man grabbed at a phone and punched in numbers. "I have a man here who says we've a national emergency." Less than two minutes later, a young man appeared in the doorway as three police cars pulled up in front of the hotel. Six police officers spilled out and into the hotel.

Dan addressed the hotel manager and the sergeant-in-charge and filled them in on the situation. The sergeant nodded, indicating they should continue their talk out of earshot. "We received word fifteen minutes ago to be on the lookout on the Skipton-Knaresborough Road for anyone seeking help from a disabled car. We searched the location where the disable car was supposed to be, but there was no car, so, it must have been towed…"

Dan nodded, removed his wallet and flipped it open to reveal his identification card. "I have reason to believe my partner is a hostage of Eric Sykes."

The police sergeant grunted in disbelief. "Doctor Sykes? Director of Nano-Comp U.K.? How could a respectable man such has he be involved in such a thing as you say?"

"That's what I intend to find out." Dan returned his wallet to his pocket and flipped his cell phone open, brought the listener on the other end up to date, then passed the phone to the Sergeant.

The sergeant wilted as he listened. "Yes. Yes. Of course. I understand. We will give him all our support." When the call ended, Dan took his phone from the sergeant who, white-faced, continued. "Whitehall has ordered a platoon of military police and troops from the nearest garrison. My orders are to provide you with anything…"

Dan grunted. "What Garrison? From where? More than half the garrisons in the UK have closed down."

"Claro Barracks, maybe ten miles away by air."

"Call them. Have them join us at Nano Comp U.K. We've no time to waste. All I can tell you is that I must resolve this situation with all possible haste."

Dan rode with the sergeant in the sergeant's police car. They were accompanied by one second police car. As they speed through the darkness and out of town, Dan rasped, "How far is it?" tired, hungry and worried he had let Kate down.

"About five miles," the sergeant replied. "The army is sending a platoon of Special Forces: This must be a really big 'situation' for them to do that."

"It is," replied Dan succinctly. The police sergeant wanted

to know more but knew better than to ask. He would find out soon enough.

The rain slackened to a drifting mist as the two police cars sped across a small stone bridge and into the parking lot of Nano Comp UK. The building had once been an old Woolen mill located over Skipton's busiest canal, the canal serving as a primary means of transport for the woolen industry in its heyday. Now, all that remained was the substantial stone building with its imposing mill chimney, tall and tower-like. Many such old mills had been renovated into office buildings often with living quarters, which was exactly what Sykes had done.

Light streamed from the double glass doors leading into the new main entrance. Sykes, at his desk on the top floor, heard a soft chime and glanced at the custom 400-inch flat screen that occupied an entire wall of his office. The advanced 225K picture showed two police cars driving up and stopping outside in defensive position. He signaled to Kate to sit. His "public office," was located in floors one through eleven beneath the private heliport of the 12-story structure. Sykes claimed the top floor as his executive office, and the old mill and its adjoining chimney as his private office and laboratory. With eleven floors of computer scientists and technicians hard at work seven days a week, only his secretary and he knew of the two-person pneumatic lift installed inside the massive chimney stack, its secret entrance hidden located within his private office in case he needed to leave the complex quickly and unseen. The rest of the personnel and any guests used the glass elevator in the foyer.

A. G. Hayes

Chapter 32

Gwen and Chadron edged forward in the security line at Rome's Fiumicino Airport, both dressed head to foot in black *burqas*. Gwen could both hear and feel her breath as it exited through the tight face mesh. For a moment, she wondered how Arab women, dressed similarly in black were able to bear the heat of the Middle East. Glancing at Chadron, Gwen saw a typical, self-contained Islamic woman. When the number of couples ahead of them reduced to one, she felt her heart speed up in anticipation. Behind Gwen and Chadron trailed one wheeled carry-on each. When it was their turn, a burly official pawed through their luggage and satisfied, placed it on a conveyer belt, roughly jerked his head in a bored, "move on" signal toward the body-sized metal detector.

Gwen went first. She raised her arms shoulder high as instructed while the unit scanned her body, and breathed a silent sigh of relief when the official waved her forward and out.

Standing aside, she watched as Chadron approached the metal detector, and held her breath as she witnessed the breakthrough in robotic design as the scanner finished its job and the official waved on Chadron. Chadron's "skin" was Gwen's own design. For all anyone there knew, Chadron was just another Muslim tourist. As the two walked toward their gate, Gwen whispered softly, "Chadron, we just made history."

Like most metropolitan airports around the world, there was a constant flow of people. Few looked as relaxed as the thin man in a black raincoat seated on a bench facing the main concourse. Instinctively, Gwen knew the man was a watcher. In fact, she was partially correct. There were three. The other two were Louise and Grainger.

The powers at 68 Via Condotti had readily agreed to Grainger's suggestion of a meeting to discuss his and Louise's plans for a "working" retirement. Within hours, the two octogenarians were in Rome, sitting in Father Enrico Conti's room of The Academy of Science building in the Vatican gardens. While changes in Vatican procedures typically took years, sometimes centuries, the Jesuit enclave of SIV was more up to date, and Fr. Conti, when contacted by Louise Zander, was already well aware of the two's formidable backgrounds.

"Madam Zander. It is a pleasure to once again welcome you to the Vatican. It has been too long since we last saw each other."

Grainger Milburn's eyes flicked between the two; he had no idea they'd met before.

Louise smiled.

Conti, noting Grainer's surprise, said, "Yes. We first met when you were still at the Institute Surval if I recall."

"The Surval Monteux," Louise acknowledged dreamily, adding softly, "I do not count years anymore, Father. Takes too long, and I have none left to waste."

Fr. Conti nodded and picked up the crystal pyramid he kept on his desk. "Do you remember this?" As he turned it in his hand, shafts of light struck different internal angles, flashing vivid colors about them like a rainbow.

Louise nodded. "Of course. Daphne sent it to you a few years after the war; I delivered it to you myself."

Grainger listened, eyes widening.

Conti smiled seeing Grainger's increasing surprise, and addressed him directly. "When you and Louise went your separate ways after the Cold War, I contacted her through Daphne Delferholm in London. We have been in touch ever since."

Grainger was stunned.

"Don't worry, Grainger," Louise said softly. "I am sure you have done a few things since the war that I know little about, also."

"Yes, well, I mean…but *you* working for the SIV!"

"Part-time contract-stuff mostly."

Fr. Conti added, "Louise, a celebrated academician and writer, and you, Mr. Milburn, her dedicated companion, both involved in things most secret. I assume a contract between SIV and the two of you together would be of interest?"

Granger smiled, fumbled for his pipe and tobacco, and slowly packed the bowl.

Chapter 33

Louise sat humped in a wheelchair, two pieces of carry-on luggage on her lap, an airport attendant pushing her while Grainger walked shakily beside her, cane in hand.

What a wondrous age of intrigue we live in, when intelligence agents covering as old age pensioners can work side-by-side with no one suspecting the two. In fact, modern language had evolved to the point where many counter-intelligence operatives would likely not even understand what the two were saying to each other, period. Grainger lagged behind allowing the wheelchair to plow a path throughout the throngs of busy passengers, thinking that he would have to see to it they both had wheels next time.

The wheelchair attendant placed them close to their departure gate with the assurance that someone would see them boarded safely along with the other early boarders. Louise rummaged through her handbag, removed a pack of cigarettes and attempted to light up, only to be politely informed by a nearby gate attendant that smoking was not openly permitted in the airport. At a signal from Louise, an assistant attendant wheeled her into a small cubicle marked "Smoking Permitted." "Here we are on our first assignment, Grainger. And, as always, it pays to know the right people."

Chapter 34

The sullen oppressive heat of Mumbai, India, contrasted sharply with the icy air-conditioned conference room at Pashagora International. Two East Indian men in business suits and a red-haired European woman in her mid-thirties dressed in an emerald blue sari sat around the highly polished conference table. One of the men poured himself a glass of water and sipped slowly at it. The colorful tableau was awaiting the arrival of Kumar Pashagora, President and Chief Executive Officer.

The slim redhead in the blue sari, while employed by the British Museum as a Professor of Vatican Antiquities, had studied the writings of a Father Pittau, "courtesy of the Vatican Secret Service." Several years ago, the Vatican had held an in-depth study of Women in the Church that had catapulted her into a world unimaginable to even the most extreme feminist ten years before.

She was born in an orphanage in Rome, indistinguishable

from all the other orphans except for her red-hair and blue-eyes. As time passed, the nuns noticed that she had an additional trait of interest: She was extraordinarily smart. A fast learner bordering on genius at two years of age, by the age of three, the Sisters contacted the Vatican about her. The Vatican, realizing they had a child prodigy in their hands, made use of the resource at once, enrolling her in the best of schools where she seemingly inhaled the most difficult lessons with unparalleled ease and speed.

There being no public record of her place of birth nor the education she received under various Vatican-assigned pseudonyms, she was clearly "destined for great things" as her instructors and caretakers were wont to say. As a young woman, she attended high school in Switzerland, a finishing school in England and, when ready, was wisked off to Cambridge University. An exceptionally well educated, Vatican controlled "English" woman given the field name, Amanda Fox, she quickly became a treasured agent within the SIV.

Amanda straightened in her chair as the door swished open and Kumar Pashagora entered dressed in a dark blue, double-breasted Savile Row suit. Pashagora looked the perfect Indian Englishman, down to his highly polished, black, Wildsmith loafers. He had an affinity for all things British from his days at Eton and Cambridge back in the in the age of the Raj.

A handsome man now in his late seventies, Kumar's aura of command had not faded despite his busy and oftentimes mysterious life, and he had retained his legendary ability to enchant women with a single glance. Power, riches and good health had been useful assets to the crafty, sly, notorious person he was inside. The world was his toy and he knew it.

"Ah, Miz Fox. We are delighted to see you. We hope the flight from London was uneventful?" He knew it had been, seeing as she had been flown to the meeting in one of his private long-distance jets.

Amanda caught the almost imperceptible flicker in Pashagora's eyes that to those trained in interrogation indicated the deep cunning of a sociopathic liar. An icy chill inside her caused goose bumps to erupt on both her arms. Quickly, she rubbed them away.

Pashagora, observing her closely, displayed a look of concern and asked, "Too chilly for you, Miz Fox?"

"Thank you, Mister Pashagora. I am fine."

"My mother used to say that happens when someone walks across his or her grave. An old wives' tale, no doubt left over from the British Raj."

Settling into his red leather chair, an enormous affair designed to make even the most bombastic visitor feel small when seated across the table, Pashagora placed his hands on the ivory inlay of the conference table where only he sat.

Legend had it the inlay had taken the ivory of fourteen bull elephants to construct. Amanda instantly recognized the power game he was playing. Her innate intelligence and Vatican training had taught her spycraft *par excellence*.

One of the two men pushed back his chair, stood, squared his shoulders, faced Pashagora and smiled thinly. "Your son has decided it is time for a change of guard." Like a trained actor on a movie-set, the man slid his hand inside his belt and withdrew a 3-D printed, perfectly weighted, white plastic throwing knife, hitting Pashagora between the eyes. One throw. Instant death.

Turning toward Amanda, the killer said, "You were invited here to bear witness, Amanda Fox. Your immediate return to London will be by the same means as you arrived." The killer turned on heel, walked around the conference table to the slumped body and with a swift movement pulled the knife from Pashagora's face and cut the ring finger from his hand. "His son requested this as proof. Be sure it gets to him." She steeled herself as the man passed her the finger in a bloodied handkerchief.

Chapter 35

Grainger and Louise were both looking forward to their first assignment briefing in London with Fr. Conroy at a place where they would liaise in future endeavors involving almost anything dealing with artificial intelligence, human or otherwise.

Louise sighed. "Shelly summarized it so well: 'The white radiance of eternity'. We know it now by the name 'Deep Mind'. Logically speaking, Deep Mind or something like it will eventually control and quite possibly own everything."

Grainger nodded his agreement. "But who will control and own Deep Mind?" he asked, repacking his pipe. "That is the question."

After passing successfully through airport security, Gwen and Chadron were whisked across London by MI-5 to Deep Mind. Gwen took a moment in the car to switch Chadron to hibernation mode, wondering what Chadron's own future would be in all that was happening.

A. G. Hayes

Chapter 36

Kate, umbrella across her knees, sat grimly in Sykes' Skipton office. She had come to the decision that AI in all its potentially different manifestations had successfully moved from theory and research into the arena of application whether she or anyone liked it or not. Being conscious meant that humans, in order to survive as such, would have to become aware and remain vigilant of everything AI that was or could potentially become conscious.

At this moment, however, nearly every person on earth was still living blindly in the past. Traditional scientists would continue to advance the traditional sciences, leaving world governments corporations like JLB, Nano-Comp U.K., Pashagora International and Tolomeo Technics and the Vatican to decide the future of the human race. Only one thing was certain: That future would be unlike anything humanity had ever known.

The world had exited the incredibly short Anthropocene

Age of uniquely human impact on the world and silently entered the age of Artificial Intelligence, long before learning how to control either. The pre-industrial age in which most of humanity was still living was fast vanishing, destined to be erased with little if any attention to right or wrong, moral or immoral, good or evil. In the AI era, questions could be expected to be directed straight at the logical root of any problem and solved with collective AI meta-consciousness, immediately moving on to the next question, all without any necessary human context.

"You seem in another world." Sykes' voice startled Kate. Before she could reply, a voice from security announced over the intercom that the Police were downstairs demanding to speak to him.

"Tell them to wait. Tell them I'm on a long distance conference call." Sykes picked up the automatic pistol on his desk, pushed back his desk chair and ordered Kate to follow him. She did, wondering what was next.

"Come! We have to move fast!" Scooping papers from the center desk drawer into a briefcase, he headed across the room to what looked like a blank wall. Sykes pressed a portion of the wall and it slid to one side, revealing a small, two-person cage.

"Get in," Sykes ordered, brandishing his weapon, pushing her forward. As he followed, the door hissed closed and smoothly and silently descended without a sound. "We have places to go, and I need you."

Kate remained silent as the musty smell of mud and old vegetation seeped into the lowering carriage. In less than thirty seconds, there was a slight bump, then the door hissed open. The musty, cellar-like odor now hung heavy in the air.

"Get out," Sykes snapped. Holding the briefcase and pistol in one hand, he removed and activated a flashlight in the other and swung the beam around what appeared to be a drab space with an earthen floor. Crossing to a wall, he touched a hidden switch and the interior lit dimly by way of a low wattage bulb revealing an outer, bricked, whitewashed, perimeter wall. Kate slumped against the wall, her fingers white as she gripped the shaft of her umbrella. Could she bring herself to trigger the hidden switch and plunge the steel blade into Sykes, ending this brilliant but demented man's life?

"They can't get through this chimney wall easily, and by the time they figure out how, we'll have escaped and be far away. Now listen carefully and do exactly as I say: The inside of this chimney is forty-five feet wide. That leaves six feet between this wall and the outer wall of the stack. I will open a hidden door, and lower a rope ladder that will take us to the banks of Skipton canal. We have plenty of time, so we can descend slowly. You first, Kate."

The descent down the rope proved dicey. Moisture driven

by tunnel wind made the ladder cold, wet and slick. Kate fumbled briefly and dropped the umbrella. It fell straight down, plunging into a soft muddy bank, its curved handle facing upward. Seconds later they were both on the ground and Kate had recovered her umbrella.

Sykes wasted no time, "Stay close and follow me. The canal is just ahead."

The rain outside had increased to an almost opaque, slanting sheet, and a cold wet wind pierced through her clothing. Kate stumbled across a hassock of thick grass, trying her best to keep sight of Sykes ahead of her.

Sykes stopped abruptly in mid-stride. "We're there. Come here beside me and stay still. Not a sound, understand?"

Kate grunted in agreement. She wanted to be out of danger as much he did.

Sykes aimed the flashlight forward into the darkness, and flipped the switch quickly on and off. The entire movement took less than a second. A moment later he said quizzically, "He has us. Keep walking forward."

Rising from the grass a tall, thin man appeared. "All's ready, boss. Follow me." Within three steps they were standing beside a blacked out canal barge, the thin man offering a hard bony hand to Kate. "Step down and mind your head."

Kate moved slowly down a stepladder-like boarding staircase. Inside, the barge smelled stale and unused. Sykes, following, flipped a switch and the cabin lit up weakly; just enough for him to do a quick inspection. "Make sure the curtains stay closed. No light must show outside; we have, after all, company adamantly looking for us not too far away. We'll use the electric motor the first three miles down the canal so no one hears us."

With the quiet hum of from electric motor, the barge pulled away from the bank into the middle of the canal. The thin man knew his job. Locating and installing an electric motor large enough to soundlessly drive the longboat had been a tough job. None of the barge builders could understand the his need. Well, perhaps a couple would have, if he had been inclined to tell them.

The longboat moved with grace and silence, easing down the dark water of the Leeds and Liverpool canal, taking them further and further from the frantic efforts of their pursuers.

Sykes began nervously pacing the small cabin, checking in cupboards and drawers as he did. Kate sat in the cabin watching him pace and search. It seemed so out of character.

A. G. Hayes

Chapter 37

The army detachment, Dan, and the police had finished searching all twelve floors of offices without success. Sykes Land Rover was still parked out front. Dan had chased the man across the moors to this office. Where in hell could he have gone? Like that artificial intelligence hellion that had almost killed him in the greenhouse, Sykes had vanished into thin air.

"Sir!" An army officer appeared at Dan's side. "We've deployed our infrared scanner and are getting higher than expected readings from within the old factory chimney."

A major joined the group. "We can break through the chimney wall if you order us to. We're on a government operation; the sky is the limit."

"Do it," Dan replied without thinking.

The major waved to his men and everyone headed for the old smokestack. A special army vehicle braked to a halt adjacent to chimney and a half dozen men began unloading equipment. "We'll have a hole in that stack in no time," the

Major said. "Do you really think Sykes may be hiding in there?

"He may. If so, my partner may be in there, too," Dan said.

Chapter 38

In a small compact office beneath the busy streets of Piccadilly London, Gwen and a rebooted Chadron sat facing a male official of SkyVault, a little-known research operation dedicated to critically defining the nature of artificial intelligence self-developed by conscious artificially intelligent machines and humanoids.

"We appreciate you joining us…" Jason Elderberry, a rheumy-eyed interrogator began in a sarcastic voice.

Gwen bristled. "We were brought here without being told why, and I have several questions that need to be answered before we 'join' anything, understand?"

"No, I do not." Elderberry looked sharply at the two. "Not, that is, until we have all *our* questions answered." A knock caused them all to turn toward the door. "Who is it?" Elderberry's voice sounded agitated as if the interruption were a capital crime.

"Saunders, Sir. And it is important. Everyone is needed

upstairs at once. Sir Ralph is in a blue funk over a message he just received from Rome." In a hushed voice, Sanders added, "The Pope has gone missing." The three sitting around the interrogation table exchanged startled glances.

Elderberry's response to the news was complete disgust at having his interview postponed if not cancelled entirely.

Gwen's response was both surprise and abject horror. "Who would…?"

Chadron displayed the thinnest of smiles on her otherwise impassive face.

The door to Elderberry's office swung back and struck the wall loudly, allowing two armed military policemen to enter side by side. Others, behind them, cradled drawn automatic weapons, and took up positions obviously designed to protect and detain Gwen and Chadron. "It's starting," murmured Gwen, though exactly what "it" was was unclear to everyone in the room, except, perhaps Chadron.

The shock swept through the Vatican like a tsunami. In the Vatican Gardens, retired Pope Benedict's house was immediately surrounded by Swiss Guards skirted by armed military vehicles, a scene undreamed of in past times.

While the news about the missing pope was being digested by the media, Dan was asserting his authority to be among the first through the jagged, gaping hole the army had punched in the side of the chimney.

Dust swirled thickly inside. The army immediately began directing their tactical LED torches into the dust and darkness. Inside the circular brick chimney, shadows began appearing alongside the searchers' darting flashlight beams. In a few minutes, it was apparent there was no one inside the chimney area other than the search team.

While the world gasped at the news of the pope's disappearance, social media began circulating theories as to how and to where he could vanish so fast. Pundits of all kinds scooped up conspiratorial social media postings and took to the international airwaves, enlarging on them, adding their weight to one or another. Twelve hours after the first announcement, there were literally hundreds of conspiracy theories, but still no definite answers; the pope, the head of the Catholic Church, leader of billions, officially became a missing person.

Newspaper headlines changed minute by minute as information poured in from all around the world. The only new details, however, were that when the pope's personal assistant had entered his room, number 201 at the Domus Sanctae Marthae, he found the room empty, the pope's slippers lying neatly on the floor at his bedside. As a side note, most of the world believed the Pope lived in a private apartment in the Vatican, which, in fact, was once true. However, by choice, this pope had moved to less grand accommodations outside the actual Vatican. That and his surprise disappearance lent credence to what some were claiming was the start of the end of times—the long anticipated Christian "Rapture"—which the rest of the world was slowly coming to call the "Realization."

Chapter 39

After a while, Sykes cautiously turned on the long canal barge's single navigation light and the radio. The usual night music was interrupted with a news flash announcing the Pope's disappearance then returned to the music it had interrupted. Sykes stared forward into the darkness momentarily pondering the fate of the missing Pope then returned his attention back to his own situation. Checking his watch, he said to his assistant, "We'll be at number three turning basin on the edge of town in about five minutes. Drop us off there, then turn around and double back. Keep going all the way back to Liverpool. If stopped by authorities asking questions, advise them the barge is being returned to home base for a refit. It's a good excuse as this is the time of the year when most of the pleasure barges are refitted in anticipation of the summer crowds wanting to hire them for summer vacation."

A. G. Hayes

Chapter 40

Five days later, Rome was still a city in shock. The sudden loss of the leader of one of the largest international businesses in the world had pushed the entire world off balance. Church officials were called to 24-hour-a-day duty. The Pope, in absentia, became a man who, as a five-year veteran peacemaker during one of the most troubled times in papal history, had been awarded the respect of every decent world citizen, Catholic or not. More and more were suggesting that, like the prophet Elijah, he might have been swept up bodily by God into heaven without suffering death; others had begun calling upon his name for miracles. At the same time, some, mainly outside the Church, had begun villifying him, suggesting he was an alien called back by his race after having accomplished his nepharious assignment to divide the world, person against person, in the manner of the prophesied anti-Christ.

In a small, well-appointed office on the third floor at 68

Via Condotti, several serious looking men in dark suits seated themselves around a shiny oval table. Others present stationed themselves around the table where an elderly man in an out-of-date suit sat, a worried look on his face.

If you enjoyed *68 Via Condotti: Book 1 - Eternity Ltd.* consider the first book in A. G. Hayes' Koski and Falk series, *Who's Killing All the Lawyers?*

Lawyers are being murdered by laser-driven arrows. The FBI believes that someone is training Native Americans to take over the US economic system. Joe Falk and Susan Koski are assigned to find the hired killer and The Fox, the real force behind the killings.

GREAT SOUTHWEST BOOK FESTIVAL AWARD
AMAZON KINDLE GENRE BESTSELLER

…the second in the Koski and Falk series, *The Judas List:*

A 700-year-old prayer book, a key and a faded blueprint came to light and begin a search for Nazi Herman Goering's treasure. In modern day Vienna, American agents Koski and Falk must locate the treasure and the Judas List—a compendium of individuals and organizations that financed WWII, and intend to bring about the Fourth Reich.
PACIFIC RIM BOOK FESTIVAL AWARD

…the third book in the Falk and Koski adventure series, *Imminent Danger* by A. G. Hayes.

Jamul, an adored American pop singer, dreams of a grand show of Islamic Jihad power, intending to use a biological weapon to eradicate religious leaders at an Easter service at the Hollywood Bowl. Cerberus agents Joe Falk and Susan Koski must stop the next brutal terrorist attack on American soil.

LA BOOK FESTIVAL AWARD

…the fourth in the multi-award-winning Koski and Falk series, *The Chemical Factor*:

A stolen weapon of mass destruction hidden years ago on board the Queen Mary has remained there undisturbed. Up to now. Agents Falk and Koski are called in to evacuate the ship and somehow locate the bomb. Risking their lives to locate the weapon, they discover that a Girl Scout has strayed from her group during evacuation and is hiding in the ship.

PACIFIC RIM BOOK FESTIVAL AWARD

…the fifth in the multi-award-winning Koski and Falk series and first in the Kate Keenan Special Assignment Series, *Quantum Death*:

Koski and Falk come up against what very well may prove to be their most complex and dangerous case yet: The Quantum Death Machine. Each faces mortal peril, while, at the same time, their smoldering relationship begins to heat up.

AMSTERDAM BOOK FESTIVAL AWARD

…the second in the Kate Keenan Special Assignment Series, *Finding Kate*:

Long-ignored computer genius Kate Keenan has designed a computer program that will put Hollywood and Bollywood out of business overnight. Suddenly everyone wants her...and her program. Kate struggles to keep ahead of a lethal hoard of pursuers with only one thing in mind: FINDING KATE and possessing or destroying the program.

…A. G. Hayes' unusual departure into 1940's comic Vaudeville with *CHANG the Magic Cat* an innovative screenplay-novel:

A rollicking, adventurous screenplay-novel set in merry old England that follows Chang, the wise, mystical, magical, all-knowing cat through his adventures with bumbling humans as they search to discover the rightful heir to Briersly Manor.

…the sixth in the multi-award-winning Koski and Falk series:
The Solar Triangle:

Agent Susan Koski swept her binoculars across the dark sea and focused on the Flangenan Lighthouse, that had clung tenaciously to the rocky outcroppings of Tiree Island for over one hundred years. Then she noticed the group of black-clad soldiers, weapons drawn, silently encircling the lighthouse…in their sixth adventure, Koski and Falk face what may be one of their most deadly assignments yet: Operation Solar Triangle.

A. G. Hayes

About the Author

Multi-award-winning author A. G. Hayes studied television writing at UCLA, and published short fiction for CBS TV and other television production companies. He lives in the Sierra Nevada Foothills and spends his time writing and traveling to nearly every part of the world. He uses personal experiences gained during his service with British intelligence in Eastern Europe and the Middle East to enrich the characters of his protagonist teams. He is the multi-award-winning author of *Who's Killing All the Lawyers* (Savant 2011), *The Judas List* (Savant 2012), *Imminent Danger* (Savant 2013), *The Chemical Factor* (Savant 2015), *Quantum Death* (Savant 2016), *Finding Kate* (Savant 2016), *The Solar Triangle* (Savant 2017), and *CHANG the Magic Cat* (Savant 2017).

A. G. Hayes

If you enjoyed *68 VIA CONDOTTI: Book 1 - Eternity Ltd.,* consider these other fine books from Savant Books and Publications:

Essay, Essay, Essay by Yasuo Kobachi
Aloha from Coffee Island by Walter Miyanari
Footprints, Smiles and Little White Lies by Daniel S. Janik
The Illustrated Middle Earth by Daniel S. Janik
Last and Final Harvest by Daniel S. Janik
A Whale's Tale by Daniel S. Janik
Tropic of California by R. Page Kaufman
Tropic of California (the companion music CD) by R. Page Kaufman
The Village Curtain by Tony Tame
Dare to Love in Oz by William Maltese
The Interzone by Tatsuyuki Kobayashi
Today I Am a Man by Larry Rodness
The Bahrain Conspiracy by Bentley Gates
Called Home by Gloria Schumann
Kanaka Blues by Mike Farris
First Breath edited by Z. M. Oliver
Poor Rich by Jean Blasiar
The Jumper Chronicles by W. C. Peever
William Maltese's Flicker by William Maltese
My Unborn Child by Orest Stocco
Last Song of the Whales by Four Arrows
Perilous Panacea by Ronald Klueh
Falling but Fulfilled by Zachary M. Oliver
Mythical Voyage by Robin Ymer
Hello, Norma Jean by Sue Dolleris
Richer by Jean Blasiar
Manifest Intent by Mike Farris
Charlie No Face by David B. Seaburn
Number One Bestseller by Brian Morley
My Two Wives and Three Husbands by S. Stanley Gordon
In Dire Straits by Jim Currie
Wretched Land by Mila Komarnisky
Chan Kim by Ilan Herman
Who's Killing All the Lawyers? by A. G. Hayes
Ammon's Horn by G. Amati
Wavelengths edited by Zachary M. Oliver
Almost Paradise by Laurie Hanan
Communion by Jean Blasiar and Jonathan Marcantoni

68 Via Condotti: Book One - Eternity Ltd.

The Oil Man by Leon Puissegur
Random Views of Asia from the Mid-Pacific by William E. Sharp
The Isla Vista Crucible by Reilly Ridgell
Blood Money by Scott Mastro
In the Himalayan Nights by Anoop Chandola
On My Behalf by Helen Doan
Traveler's Rest by Jonathan Marcantoni
Keys in the River by Tendai Mwanaka
Chimney Bluffs by David B. Seaburn
The Loons by Sue Dolleris
Light Surfer by David Allan Williams
The Judas List by A. G. Hayes
Path of the Templar—Book 2 of The Jumper Chronicles by W. C. Peever
The Desperate Cycle by Tony Tame
Shutterbug by Buz Sawyer
Blessed are the Peacekeepers by Tom Donnelly and Mike Munger
The Bellwether Messages edited by D. S. Janik
The Turtle Dances by Daniel S. Janik
The Lazarus Conspiracies by Richard Rose
Purple Haze by George B. Hudson
Imminent Danger by A. G. Hayes
Lullaby Moon (CD) by Malia Elliott of Leon & Malia
Volutions edited by Suzanne Langford
In the Eyes of the Son by Hans Brinckmann
The Hanging of Dr. Hanson by Bentley Gates
Flight of Destiny by Francis Powell
Elaine of Corbenic by Tima Z. Newman
Ballerina Birdies by Marina Yamamoto
More More Time by David B. Seabird
Crazy Like Me by Erin Lee
Cleopatra Unconquered by Helen R. Davis
Valedictory by Daniel Scott
The Chemical Factor by A. G. Hayes
Quantum Death by A. G. Hayes and Raymond Gaynor
Big Heaven by Charlotte Hebert
Captain Riddle's Treasure by GV Rama Rao
All Things Await by Seth Clabough
Tsunami Libido by Cate Burns
Finding Kate by A. G. Hayes
The Adventures of Purple Head, Buddha Monkey and Sticky Feet by Erik and Forest Bracht
In the Shadows of My Mind by Andrew Massie

A. G. Hayes

The Gumshoe by Richard Rose
In Search of Somatic Therapy by Setsuko Tsuchiya
Cereus by Z. Roux
The Solar Triangle by A. G. Hayes
Shadow and Light edited by Helen R. Davis
A Real Daughter by Lynne McKelvey
StoryTeller by Nicholas Bylotas
Bo Henry at Three Forks by Daniel Bradford
One Night in Bangkok by Keith Rees
Kindred edited by Doc Krinberg
Cleopatra Victorious by Helen R. Davis

Navel of the Sea by Elizabeth McKague

Coming Soon:
Books 2 and 3 in the 3-part *68 Via Condotti* serial by A. G. Hayes

Talking Story: Storytelling Meets Phonomenology by Jamie Dela Cruz
Crowned Rose of York: An Alternative History in Two Volumes by Carolina Casas
Truth and Tell Travel the Solar System by Helen R. Davis
Honeymoon Forever: Find Love, Keep Love by R. Page Kaufman
Short Beach: Memento Mori by Kenneth M. Kapp

68 Via Condotti: Book One - Eternity Ltd.

and from Aignos Publishing, an *avant garde* imprint of Savant Books and Publications:

The Dark Side of Sunshine by Paul Guzzo
Happy that it's Not True by Carlos Aleman
Cazadores de Libros Perdidos by German William Cabasssa Barber [Spanish]
The Desert and the City by Derek Bickerton
The Overnight Family Man by Paul Guzzo
There is No Cholera in Zimbabwe by Zachary M. Oliver
John Doe by Buz Sawyers
The Piano Tuner's Wife by Jean Yamasaki Toyama
Nuno by Carlos Aleman
An Aura of Greatness by Brendan P. Burns
Polonio Pass by Doc Krinberg
Iwana by Alvaro Leiva
University and King by Jeffrey Ryan Long
The Surreal Adventures of Dr. Mingus by Jesus Richard Felix Rodriguez
Letters by Buz Sawyers
In the Heart of the Country by Derek Bickerton
El Camino De Regreso by Maricruz Acuna [Spanish]
Diego in Two Places by Carlos Aleman
Prepositions by Jean Yamasaki Toyama
Deep Slumber of Dogs by Doc Krinberg
Saddam's Parrot by Jim Currie
Beneath Them by Natalie Roers
Chang the Magic Cat by A. G. Hayes
Illegal by E. M. Duesel
Island Wildlife: Exiles, Expats and Exotic Others by Robert Friedman
The Winter Spider by Doc Krinberg
The Princess in My Head by J. G. Matheny

Coming Soon:
Comic Crusaders by Richard Rose